CAKES FOR THE QUEEN OF HEAVEN

D0011477

CAKES FOR THE QUEEN OF HEAVEN

AN EXPLORATION OF WOMEN'S POWER PAST PRESENT AND FUTURE

SHIRLEY ANN RANCK

delphi press

DELPHI PRESS, INC.,
CHICAGO, ILLINOIS

Published 1995 by Delphi Press, Inc., Chicago, IL.

ISBN 1-878980-10-6

Library of Congress Catalogue Number 93-73573

99 98 97 96 95 94   5 4 3 2 1

Grateful acknowledgement is made to The Unitarian Universalist Association for permission to use material published in the original curriculum entitled *Cakes for the Queen of Heaven*.

Contents

In memory of my mother
Ann West Bush,
because "I am her only novel."

Acknowledgements

BECAUSE THIS BOOK IS BASED upon the course *Cakes for the Queen of Heaven* I would like to express again my appreciation for the important contributions made by several women during the time the course was first developed: The Reverend Leslie A. Westbrook, first editor of the course who worked with me on the early design of the sessions; Elizabeth Anastos, editor of the course, for her enormous patience and educational expertise; the Reverend Emily Champagne for much of the initial research; the Reverend Elinor Artman for her poems; Rabbi Susan Talve for her understanding of Midrash and her workshop design based on that understanding; Rosemary Matson for her early support and encouragement; my friend and crony Chris Bailey for countless hours of discussion and clarification of many issues in feminist thealogy.

The many women who took the course and then wrote or spoke to me about their enjoyment of it and its impact on their lives deserve my special thanks. They affirmed and empowered me; and they welcomed me into their circles, their conferences, their retreats and their homes. They motivated me to begin and complete this book. One group at the White Bear Unitarian Universalist Fellowship in Minnesota, even raised money for me which helped me visit some of the Goddess sites in Greece!

My thanks go to the women who worked on changing this book from a computer disk to an actual book. Chris Harnesk, the designer of this book, and Colleen Koziara, who drew the cover illustration made this book into its beautiful self. My special thanks also to Liz Davidson for her careful editing and encouragement as well as her special Pagan presence all along the way.

Most importantly, I thank Karen Jackson of Delphi Press, not only for her ceaseless encouragement and patience in helping me through the publication process but also for her warm friendship and supportive presence even before the process began.

Bright Blessings to all!

—Shirley Ann Ranck
Berkeley, California
October 1993

Acknowledgment is made to the following for permission to reprint their works:

Elinor Artman, *Between Two Gods*, © 1979 Elinor Artman; Marge Piercy for the poems, *A Work of Artiface*, © 1979 by Marge Piercy, and *My Mother's Novel*, © 1979 by Marge Piercy; Ellen Bass, for *First Menstruation*, © 1979 Ellen Bass, and *For My Mother*, © 1979 Ellen Bass; Starhawk, *The Charge of the Goddess* and *The Declaration of the Four Sacred Things*. Illustrations by Leo Morrissey, Courtesy of Star River Productions.

"Do you not see what they do in the cities of Judah and in the streets of Jerusalem? The children gather wood and the fathers kindle the fire, and the women knead the dough to make cakes to the Queen of Heaven, and they pour out libations to other gods, in order to anger me!"

— *Jeremiah 7:17-18*

"As for the word that you have spoken to us in the name of Yahweh—we shall not listen to you. But we shall without fail to do everything as we said: we shall burn incense to the Queen of Heaven, and shall pour her libations as we used to do...in the cities of Judah, in the streets of Jerusalem. For then we had plenty of food, and we were all well and saw no evil. But since we ceased burning incense to the Queen of Heaven and to pour her libations, we have wanted everything and have been consumed by sword and famine."

—*Jeremiah 44: 16-18*

Preface

IN 1986 THE UNITARIAN UNIVERSALIST Association published a ten session course I had written called *Cakes for the
Queen of Heaven*.[1] This was for me the culmination of a long
journey into women's religious history and the relationship
between that history and important social and psychological
issues in my life as a woman.

For many years I had been consumed by a passion to
know my female religious roots—mythic Goddesses of the
Ancient Near East, strong women of ancient Judaism and in
the early Christian church, the elevation of Mary to larger-
than-life status, powerful Goddesses of Asia, Africa and the
indigenous religions of the Americas. I also wanted to know
how and why the power of the sacred Female had been
edited out of my own Western traditions.

Then I heard Carol Christ's talk "Why Women Need the
Goddess"[2] and suddenly all my training in psychology was
both drawn upon and challenged by my spiritual journey as
a woman. To imagine the Divine as female meant that my
body was sacred. To imagine the Divine as female meant that

the bond between mothers and daughters was holy, not a source of resentment or hostility. To imagine Divine power as female meant that real women like me had inherent power. To imagine the Divine will as female meant that women could act on our own behalf. I was exhilarated by these discoveries. They seemed to confirm some deep inner knowledge I had glimpsed but never quite trusted: my own competence and power, my own strength of will, my own body as a sacred source of life and nurture. I wanted other women to be empowered by these insights.

As an educator I knew that for such empowerment to take place, women had to have very personal experiences with their religious history. The course I designed was therefore both intellectual and experiential. Using small group discussion, crayons, clay and visualizations we would explore our feelings about our female bodies, our relative powerlessness in a patriarchal society, our troubled relationships with our mothers, the ways we have power taken from us or give it away every day, the images we have of ourselves, and the visions we have for our future. At the same time, with images of ancient Goddesses and Priestesses, with poetry and music, dance and discussion we would learn about the very ancient Earth Goddess, Her supreme power of creation, the mythic battles between the Goddess and the rising male gods, the ultimate loss of female power by both Goddesses and Earthly women, and the re-writing of history which tried to erase any memory of female power.

As I wrote the sessions I realized that we would in fact be retelling history from a female perspective. What would happen to us as women, I wondered, if we really absorbed that new story? What has happened has amazed me.

To open and close each session I suggested that groups light a candle and read a poem or sing a song related to the session. I encouraged women to bring their own readings or songs or pictures to share. At the time I thought it was just a good way to provide a clear beginning and ending for each session. As a humanist I did not think to call these techniques ritual. What happened in these Cakes study groups was that women began to create altars and to design elaborate and meaningful rites to express their experiences. A deep and widespread hunger for rituals relevant to modern life was discovered. Many groups designed a new style of worship service for their churches—the chairs set in concentric circles rather than rigid rows, the leadership shared. Others prodded their ministers and congregations to eliminate sexist language from their worship. In churches where the course was offered year after year to more and more women and men, ritual and worship has begun to reflect the personal and global issues of our own day: How shall women and men relate to each other as equals? How shall we in our ethnic diversity learn to respect each other? How can we come together to halt the destruction of our environment? How can we honor the sacredness of our lives and the Earth?

As I worked with the course and used it with varied groups across the continent, my own understanding of ritual deepened. I began to notice the moments, the events, the learnings that we need to celebrate and to which we can ascribe special meaning in our lives and communities. I saw that women were often healed and empowered by acts of ritual. In the process I changed. Now I take the time to light candles, bless myself with scented oils, meditate on the phases of the Moon, to acknowledge my feelings, my wonder, at both the events of my own life and the cycles of nature. And I too have been healed and put in touch with my power as a woman.

As I studied the ancient Goddesses and the Old Religions I learned that they honored the Earth as well as women. When women's groups made that discovery they often began to meet outdoors on beaches, in the woods or high on hilltops to celebrate the phases of the Moon, the Solstices, the Spring and Fall Equinoxes, reclaiming our connection to the natural world. A pressing and passionate need for such connectedness was uncovered. Both women and men became advocates for the environment.

As a mostly urban person, I was shocked to find myself in a Midwest meadow doing a spiral dance in the moonlight, or seated in a circle around a bonfire on a hillside overlooking San Francisco Bay. In the process I changed. I returned to the beaches of my youth, felt the pull of the ocean currents, the thrill of diving beneath a monster wave, the breathtaking beauty of a silvery path across the water to the moon. I also wept at the number of days "No Swimming" signs were placed on the beaches because pollution had reached dangerous levels. I re-discovered my personal connection with nature.

Perhaps the most satisfying result of the *Cakes for the Queen of Heaven* course for me has been the hundreds of individual women who have written or spoken to me about their personal experience with the course. Women of many ages, many levels of education, many kinds of lives, yet each in her own way has said the same thing: *It changed my life.* Some women learned to assert themselves with dominating husbands and were able to negotiate a whole new pattern for the relationship. Others found the courage to leave deeply unhappy marriages. Some women dared to make radical career changes, opening small businesses or returning to school for professional training. Many artists found a new focus for their talents in the lore of ancient Goddesses or the new-found pride in their female bodies. Many made no outward moves but experienced a positive inner shift in self-image or confidence. All felt empowered to change. As an educator, a psychologist and a minister I could hardly have dreamed of a greater tribute to the effectiveness of the course. That tribute has changed me by affirming and blessing my life.

Ritual now gives added meaning to the events of my life. Nature now calls forth my sense of wonder and awe. And the tribute so many women have paid to *Cakes for the Queen of Heaven* has affirmed me powerfully as a person. This book is an attempt to offer some of the same experiences to individual women.

Introduction

"WOMEN HAVE NO PAST, no history and no religion," wrote Simone de Beauvoir in 1949.[1] Today we know that women definitely have a rich past, an illustrious history, and a great variety of religious experience. We have been unaware of our female history because for the past twenty or more centuries the major world religions have expressed primarily male experience and views of the world and have ignored or deliberately suppressed female experience. Women have been here all along, of course, and now that we women are expanding the ranks of historians, archaeologists, and theologians, our enormous contributions to human culture and religion are finally being recognized.

Women within the traditions of Judaism and Christianity are discovering strong biblical women, pointing out biblical passages where the Divine is imaged as female, and finding feminist attitudes in the teachings of Jesus. These women are now demanding that the love and justice proclaimed by these traditions be applied to women as well as to men. Women within all the major world religions are challenging the male biases that they feel have distorted the original intent of their religions.

Other women are looking to the prepatriarchal religions of the ancient world in their search for female roots. Before the advent of the major world religions as we know them, and for a long time after their birth, human beings of all races practiced Earth-centered, woman-centered religions for many centuries. For many years, (male) archaeologists, anthropologists and theologians dismissed these religions as primitive, amoral, and of little interest. In recent years, however, archeological and anthropological findings—many made by women who are redefining their fields—have stimulated a new interest in and respect for the earlier religions of humankind. Women have been particularly interested to learn that these ancient religions revolved around a powerful Goddess who was expected to assure the health and prosperity of the people and of the Earth. What would it have been like to grow up in a world where God was a woman?

Some women claim that the Goddess religions of the Ancient Near East and Europe never really died but came down to us in the form of Witchcraft. Witchcraft? Yes! We have been trained to have the utmost contempt for the alleged superstitions and "devil worship" of Witchcraft, but this attitude reflects the male bias of the religions that took over. There is much evidence to support the theory that ancient religions were deliberately misdescribed and slandered by the Church of Rome as it struggled to gain political power over all aspects of people's lives.[2] "Superstition" and "devil worship" are certainly not accurate descriptions of contemporary Witchcraft. Women are rediscovering and seriously studying the centuries-old female lore of magic and the Goddess. Other women are exploring the indigenous religions of Africa and the Americas and finding the wealth of woman-honoring and Earth-honoring mythology only partly hidden beneath layers of patriarchal accretions.

Pluralism

Perhaps the most important religious task of the 20th century has been learning to take pluralism seriously. It has been necessary for each of us to begin to see our own tradition as one among many and to understand that no one tradition has the whole truth. Such pluralism cuts across all the old boundaries of race and nationality and gender. In the words of Luisah Teish:

> I will not wear
> your narrow racial jackets
> as the blood of many nations
> runs sweetly thru my veins.[3]

To be truly open to the insights of many traditions we must look to no authority but that of our own experience. For women, especially, to tap into the power of authentic selfhood is to be painfully aware of the myriad ways in which society works against the expression of female experience. To express that experience is to be in conflict with almost everything in society—the language, the legal system, the government, the economy, the structure of the family, and the symbolism of most world religions, all of which express and enhance the experience of males. As an important first step toward a more complete sacred truth honoring the whole of human experience, women of all races and traditions need to dig into history and hold up to light the symbols of female divinity and power. We cannot integrate male and female symbols in any religion if we have not first examined female symbols of Divine power.

Religions and their symbols change. The deities have changed before and they are changing now. In vast areas of the ancient world female deities reigned supreme for thousands of years, and only later were they superseded by male deities. The archaeological discoveries of the past thirty to forty years provide overwhelming documentation in the form of thousands of Goddess images and figurines, elaborate temples devoted to Ishtar and other powerful Goddesses, and sacred writings never before available to us.

A theme running through much of the ancient mythology from a variety of cultures is the contest for power between the Goddess and her ever more powerful son-lover. In all these myths She is ultimately either destroyed in a grand battle or tricked into giving up Her power to the male. This shift in Divine power occurred gradually, over many centuries, and during early historical times most cultures had both male and female deities, with varying amounts of power. Archaeologist Raphael Patai has suggested that the Israelites were no exception and that for many centuries Yahweh had a powerful female consort.[4]

The idea that gods and religions change is not a new one. Many years ago Harry Emerson Fosdick traced what he perceived to be the changes in Yahweh's characteristics which occur as we move from earliest biblical sources to later ones. He suggested that Yahweh is at first a tribal deity who travels from place to place with his people. Only later does he develop the quality of omnipresence. He is at first a jealous and vengeful deity, only later acquiring the attributes of mercy and love.[5] Ernst Troeltsch pointed out that a crucial part of any religion is the world view that supports and is supported by it. He traced the changes in world view that made medieval Christianity a strikingly different religion from that of the early church in the days of the Roman Empire and from the ascetic Protestantism of later times. Troeltsch concluded that the world view of ascetic Protestantism was not adequate for the twentieth century and that a new world view would mean a new formulation of religion.[6]

A Shift from Outer to Inner

We need to be aware of the world view that is emerging in this latter part of the twentieth century and the radical changes that are occurring in our concept of divinity. We are trying to come of age as human beings, to give up our childish dependence on a parental deity enthroned in a supernatural realm. But it is not enough to pronounce the patriarchal god dead. We are still faced with the ultimate questions about life and death and meaningful existence. Naomi Goldenberg suggests that what is happening is the internalization of religion, the awareness of an immanent God or Goddess within each of us, and an inner spiritual journey toward value and meaning as adults.[7] Such a transformation of religion from outer to inner makes each of us responsible for our values. It requires us to become fully aware of our personal and social situation and to articulate that experience. It gives validity to female as well as male experience. It challenges us to alter society whenever it fails to support harmony within the self, among selves, and in relation to nature.

If women really articulate the realities of their experience, they call into question the very symbolism of Judaism, Islam, Christianity, and other world religions, where that symbolism is overwhelmingly male. This is a difficult task because we have taken that male symbolism for granted and have been raised to believe it is the only symbolism that ever existed. That is why knowing of the existence of powerful as well as nurturing female images of the Divine in the ancient world is so important. We need to know that they existed and that for thousands of years both men and women found the worship of female divinity meaningful. Whatever we may call the religions of the future, if they are to take women seriously they cannot perpetuate exclusively male symbols.

A Shift from Supernatural to Natural

The suppression of women in religion and culture around the world has been closely related to the exploitation of the Earth. The Earth today is in a severe crisis because of the damage and pollution caused by human beings. Such damage and exploitation flow directly from the Christian belief that nature is fallen and sinful. Feminist thealogy[8] rejects that idea. Instead human beings are perceived as part of a natural world that has within it the potential for both good and evil. We are not automatically good or bad. We need a realistic assessment of the human potential for good and evil, but not a negative prejudging of the situation based on belief in a "higher" supernatural realm and the sinfulness of "lowly" humans. We can assert our limited but quite real freedom to discern and to choose the good.

As creatures of the natural world, we participate—in an inner, more conscious way—in the same power that resides in all of nature. To the extent that feminist thealogy perceives the Divine as "out there" as well as within, it is identified with the natural world and not with a supernatural realm. Such a concept of the Divine as immanent implies a rejection of the distortions of human civilization that result from childish dependence on the supernatural. Being in harmony with the Goddess of the natural world does not, for example, give one power over anyone or anything. The fear among some men that feminist Goddess imagery is a demand for female dominance over men is based on a concept of the Divine as supernatural, as "over and against" the natural world rather than immanent in it. To be in harmony with that kind of supernatural deity is indeed to demand "dominance over." But feminist thealogy identifies the Divine with the natural world and seeks power in harmony rather than in dominance. The shift to an understanding of nature, including ourselves, as sacred is crucial for our relationship with the Earth and an urgently needed attitude that will enable us to stop further environmental destruction.[9]

What about Judaism and Christianity?

Although Judaism and Christianity are but two among many sources of religious inspiration around the world, they are nevertheless the traditions within which most Americans are raised. However liberal or unorthodox our current beliefs, many of us have strong emotional ties to either Judaism or Christianity. Many women, therefore seek ways to reinterpret or transform these traditions so that they will be meaningful to contemporary feminists, both women and men. Elizabeth Cady Stanton pointed out many years ago, "So long as tens of thousands of Bibles are printed every year, and circulated over the whole habitable globe, and the masses in all English-speaking nations revere it as the word of God, it is vain to belittle its influence. The sentimental feelings we all have for those things we were educated to believe sacred, do not readily yield to pure reason."[10] She gathered a committee of learned women, and they produced a commentary on every biblical passage that mentions women. Stanton dryly remarked, "As all such passages combined form but one-tenth of the Scriptures, the undertaking will not be so laborious as, at the first thought, one would imagine."[11]

Today some feminist theologians insist that male scholars and clergy down through the centuries have misinterpreted and distorted the message of the biblical tradition which proclaims justice and love for all persons, male and female. The god of the Bible was at times described with female images; there were female prophets and judges; Jesus treated women with the same dignity that he did men; in the early Christian church women preached and taught and shared all responsibilities equally with men; and Paul at his best proclaimed that "in Christ there is neither male nor female." Church history is being reexamined to discover the contributions of strong women, and the writings of female mystics are being read with new interest. For women who wish to maintain their commitment to the biblical tradition there are many new approaches.

One of the most exciting discoveries in recent years has been a large collection of ancient manuscripts buried in Upper Egypt by early Christians. These writings included a number of gospels, versions of Jesus' life and work written by very early Gnostic Christians and never before available to us. Elaine Pagels[12], who has analyzed a large number of these writings, points out that Gnostic Christians used many female images to refer to the Divine, and that women had far more power and responsibility in Gnostic churches than in those that became orthodox. Another phenomenon of interest to women is that the organization of Gnostic churches appears to have been nonhierarchical and nonauthoritarian.[12] These ancient texts give strong support to the notion that the suppression of women in the Christian Church as we have known it occurred for political reasons and is a distortion of Christianity as it was known in the early churches.

As women we have a right to know all of our female religious roots, from ancient Goddesses to Witchcraft to strong women in the biblical tradition. It is up to us to relate that history to our own experience as women in the modern world and to demand that our roots and our experience be taken seriously in the formulation of new nonsexist thea/ologies. What follows is a guide for such a spiritual journey, a journey into the relationship between our ancient past and our personal experience as women.

Prologue:
How to Experience this Book

THIS BOOK IS A JOURNEY into the history, the poetry, the music, the mythology of women and religion through the ages. It is at the same time a journey into your own deepest self. You are the heroine here, the one who will journey into the depths and up to the heights of what it has meant to be a woman in the past, what it means today, and what it can mean in the future. There are questions here for you to ponder, exercises for your imagination, stories and images for you to create, strong feelings for you to experience. You should begin a journal to record your reflections and insights as you proceed.

Before reading the first chapter, find a quiet time and a space of your own. Get yourself a plump candle in an attractive holder. Light the candle and hold it in your hands. Say your name aloud, then your mother's name, her mother's name and so on, as far back as you know the names. These are your own special female ancestors. If your mother or your grandmother is still alive, have them tell you their stories and the stories they remember from their grandmothers.

Most of the stories of women's lives are not written down in history books. I have a friend who has several patchwork quilts made by her mother and grandmother. My friend can point to a certain piece of material in a quilt and say, with a chuckle, "Oh, I remember that dress..." and tell a story about the lives of the women in her family. I have a 1928 newspaper clipping with a picture of my mother directing and acting in a play. It tells me part of the story of her young life. Look around you for the stories of women in your family. They are an important part of you. Take them with you as you begin this journey. Remember them, record their lives in your journal.

Treat yourself, pamper yourself. The first luxury you must grant yourself is the luxury of time. Perhaps luxury is the wrong word. Necessity. As women, we are the caregivers, the nurturers. Time is something we do not often take for ourselves.

Allow your creativity to come forth. Make a quick visit to the craft store. Find yourself a box of crayons, some colored paper or index cards, markers, and clay. In your journal you will express yourself in words, but you can also express your feelings and insights in shape and color and form with the exercises in this book.

If you are lucky enough to have a women's bookstore in your area, pay a visit. Often they will have women's music on tapes and incense and scented oils. Choose some that appeal to you. A good bath shop will have some of these luxuries among the aromatherapy products. Use scent and candle-light to create your own sacred space.

When you are ready, in your special quiet time and place, to begin a chapter, light your candle and allow yourself to relax, to feel into the stories, the pictures, the questions. Take your time with each section. Keep a journal of your experiences. Move on at your own pace. Know that, as Nelle Morton has said, the journey is home.

ONE

Reclaiming
Our Female Bodies

LIGHT YOUR SPECIAL CANDLE and use the full power of your imagination and your feelings as you read the following visualization:

Imagine yourself standing naked before a full length mirror. Look closely at all parts of your body. Turn and look at yourself from various angles. Now look closely at your hair. What do you like about your hair? Do you like the way it looks? Do you wish for another kind of hair?

Now look at your face, your eyes, nose, mouth, skin. Do you like what you see? Now look at the rest of your body, your breasts, hips, genitals, arms, legs, your shape, your size. Are you pleased with your shape? Your size? Look carefully at your hands and feet. Do they seem attractive to you?

Now look at yourself as a whole person. How well do you like the way you look? What do you like best about your body? What do you like least about your body?

This guided visualization touches our most private experience—our feelings about our female bodies. In using the visualization with groups of women over the past ten years, it has never failed to elicit a depressing discussion of all the aspects women hate about their bodies. Only very recently have there been one or two women in any group who begin the discussion by saying "I really like my body, especially my skin (or hair or legs etc.)"

There is hardly a woman alive in this society who does not dislike something about her body. As women we learn that we are too short unless we teeter about on high heels; that we must color our hair because blondes have more fun; that we must diet until we are pencil thin; that size A breasts need the help of a padded bra or even dangerous surgery; that the hair under our arms and on our legs is unattractive and must be removed. Everything around us conveys the message that physically we are not okay as we are. We learn in subtle ways that we are inferior, an aberration from the male norm. We also learn that to be truly feminine we must look childlike, have no adult hair, and yet be able to nurture endlessly with large breasts. By the time we are grown the notion that something is wrong with the way we look is ingrained in us. Women often are so used to making themselves over into the acceptable image that they no longer notice how much they have to do to accomplish it or how beautiful they look without such props as makeup, padded bras, hair dyes, and high heels.

The indoctrination starts early. When I was six years old I became aware that my hair was straight whereas the adorable little movie star, Shirley Temple, had beautiful curls. My mother took me to the beauty shop to get a "permanent wave." In those days they put heavy pads next to the scalp, then rolled the hair up on curlers and attached metal clamps to each curler. The clamps had wires that ran to a machine and through them the hair was fried electrically for a few seconds. I was told not to dare move and I was terrified—but determined to have my curls. My fine straight hair was not good enough and had to be rejected and changed. Later on it was the color of my hair that I rejected—light brown had to be colored to become "auburn." Later still it was the gray hair that had to be colored so that I would not look "old."

When in my forties I restored my hair to its natural state, I happened to be working as a school psychologist. I was testing a little girl one day and when we had finished she asked "What color is your hair?" I said it was gray but she said "No, I mean what color is it? What is it called?" I told her that was just the way it grew. Her eyes opened wide and she said "You mean it's natural?" I think she just assumed that all women colored their hair. Looking in the mirror I didn't think salt-and-pepper gray looked that strange.

My figure of course was never good enough. Women's magazines and TV commercials are full of diet plans with pictures of very thin models. Whenever I looked in the mirror as a young woman I perceived myself as too large. In snap shots I saw myself as overweight. It was a great shock to me when I looked at those same pictures twenty years later and realized that I had actually been slim and far more attractive than I had thought earlier.

All my life I have known women who wore padded bras because they thought their breasts were too small. In recent years thousands of women have risked their health to have silicone implanted in their breasts to enlarge them. Such a risk might be worthwhile for women who have had mastectomies. To choose such a course just to fit a distorted image of femininity however seems truly tragic.

As a woman with rather wide feet and hammer toes I have always been aware of women's shoes as painful. Recently I saw enacted before my eyes the fact that women's shoes are also demeaning. I was sitting in an airport when a young couple came rushing down the corridor to board their plane at the very last minute. Airline employees were urging them to hurry as the plane was about to leave. The man broke into an easy, loping run. He wore wide, flat, comfortable shoes and covered the distance with ease. The woman tried to run but could not do more than take faster little steps. She wore three-inch spike heels and the plane just had to wait while she teetered toward the gate. Flat, comfortable shoes are still not considered attractive on a woman. I had thought we were making some progress on this matter of shoes, what with the popularity of running shoes. A few years ago I was doing some office work in downtown San Francisco and I noticed that a good many young women had climbed the business ladder to middle echelon executive positions. I watched with interest as they arrived each morning in running shoes—and then changed to high heels which they wore in the office. At lunch time they changed back to the running shoes before leaving the building. I suppose that is progress but it still seemed like a lot of trouble to maintain an image that in truth distorts and demeans.

Take a few moments now to visualize yourself as you were at the time of your first period. How did you feel about that important event? How did you feel about the changes taking place in your body? Did other people begin to treat you differently? How did you feel about that?

Menstruation is perhaps the most despised aspect of our female bodies. It is often called "the curse" and we have been taught to be embarrassed about it, or to consider ourselves physically or ritually unclean during the time of our periods. We do nothing to celebrate the beginning of this most wondrous process in the life of a young girl—the beginning of her ability to bring forth new life. As girls though we await this event with great anticipation and we long to be acknowledged as having become women. Ellen Bass describes this anticipation and longing in her poem *First Menstruation:*

I had been waiting
waiting for what felt like lifetimes.
When the first girls stayed out of the ocean
a few days a month, wore shorts instead of a swimsuit
I watched them enviously.
I even stayed out once in a while, pretending.
At last, finding blood on my panties
I carried them to my mother hoping
unsure, afraid—Mom, is this it?

She gave me Kotex and belt
showed me how to wear it.
Dot Lutz was there, smiling, saying when her Bonnie
got her period, she told her
when you have questions, come to me, ask me.
You can ask a mother anything.
I felt so strange when she said that.
Mom didn't say anything.

The three of us
standing in the bedroom
me, the woman-child, standing with the older women
and the feeling
there once was a feeling
that should be here,
there once was a rite, a communion.

I said, yes, I'll ask my mother
but we all, except maybe Dot,
knew it wasn't true.[1]

The rite or communion has not been there for us, only the "curse," another hated aspect of our female bodies. Later in our lives we also fail to honor the wisdom and power of our post-menopausal selves.

From all of these memories and observations we get a clear message: As women we are not okay as we are. There is something inherently unacceptable about our female bodies.

Imagine now a different message, a message based upon discoveries made in twentieth-century archeology and anthropology: There was a time when the female body was sacred. It was revered as the source of new life, and had the amazing ability to feed that new life. The very earliest images of the Divine were female. Because woman brought forth new life from her own body, the Divine was also imagined as female and She was believed to have created everything.

Among the Greeks, according to Charlene Spretnak, Gaia is the ancient Earth mother who brought forth the world and the human race from the "the gaping void, Chaos."[2] In the Homeric Hymn to Ge she is praised as "the oldest of divinities."

The Myth of Gaia

In the beginning there was only the great Void, only Chaos. Dancing and spinning, Gaia brought order out of Chaos. She filled the oceans, the rivers and the lakes. She pushed forth mountains and valleys and danced the plains into being. From the rolling waters and the richness of the soil She brought forth life. All that was green and growing, all that swam in the sea came from Her dancing, spinning Self. Women and men in time came forth as well.

Gaia watched over and nurtured the life she had spawned. For the women and men She sent up vapors from her steaming center at Delphi and Athens. There Her priestesses offered comfort and prophecy in response to the anxious questions people brought. The mortals made long pilgrimages to her oracles.

For millennia Gaia, the Earth-Mother, nurtured the cycles of life and death, giving birth to new life and taking back to Herself that which was stagnant and decayed. Women and men revered Gaia's cycles. They built Her temples and made offerings to Her of honey and barley cake. In the Mystery of Her Wisdom Gaia received their gifts.[3]

Feel into the knowledge that the Divine was imagined as female for many thousands of years. In the Old Stone Age the cycles of a woman's life were linked to and became the same as the cycles of Earth and sky. It was a time when small bands of human beings followed mammoth and reindeer across the land mass that is now Europe and Asia. These groups took shelter in natural caves which they decorated with beautiful and artistic designs. On the walls deep within the labyrinths they painted the animals they followed; but for their sculpture they chose the nude female.

Female figurines were carved in bone, stone or mammoth ivory. Absorb the impressive, massive shapes of these figures. Notice their great nourishing breasts and the emphasis given to the revered pubic triangle. Joseph Campbell states that the female body was experienced as a focus of Divine force, and that a system of rites was dedicated to its mystery.[4]

Yet when these sculptures were first discovered, they were dismissed as "fertility figures" by the male archaeologists and anthropologists who never for a moment considered that a female might represent the Divine.

This focus on the mystery of the Divine female continued over thousands of years from early hunter-gatherers to the neolithic farmers. In these later agricultural times a powerful Goddess known by many names presided over the fertility of the Earth as well as its people and animals. The mysteries of birth, death and the renewal of life were central to this ancient Goddess religion. She was, according to Marija Gimbutas, the Giver of Life, the Wielder of Death and the Regeneratrix.[5]

The ancient Goddess is often shown in two significant poses which recur in later historic times. In one pose Her arms are open and gracefully raised toward the sky. Stand in that pose yourself. Feel the strength, the sacred power of your own body as you lift your arms toward the Moon and the stars. The other pose is with hands cupping the breasts. Not only did the female bring forth new life from her own body, she was able to feed and sustain that life as well. In some African cultures a woman's word or oath is spoken in this pose, hands cupping or touching the sacred source of sustenance. Try speaking your truth while assuming this pose. How do you feel?

Gimbutas points out that all of these images can be viewed as aspects of one Great Goddess, analogous to Nature itself. The Goddess is immanent. She is within you as a woman. She is within the whole of her creation. No mere "fertility figure," she is the creator, sustainer and transformer of life. Nor is there any trace of a father figure in the Old Stone Age. "The life-creating power seems to have been of the Great Goddess alone."[6]

From very early times the Goddess is depicted with a snake or serpent which had the power to renew itself by shedding its skin. The serpent was one of the most wide-spread and long-lasting symbols of the life-renewing power of the Goddess. A remnant of this ancient connection between the Goddess and the serpent is found in the biblical story of Eve. Notice, however, that the symbols have been deliberately reversed. The serpent and the Goddess were transformed into negative, evil forces. How do you feel about that reversal? As you continue your journey into the roots of woman's spirituality you will encounter many such reversals.

From very early historic times through the Bronze Age, women were the primary religious and cultural leaders who founded settled economies, devised systems of language and developed the arts. It was from the Great Goddess that the first kings received their power.

In our own culture where the Divine is always spoken of in male terms and his earthly priests or representatives are male, women have been led to believe that we are not made in the image of God. We have been excluded from priesthoods because we are not male. We have come to view ourselves as aberrations from the male "norm." Modern psychological theory and research has followed the same pattern. Freudian theory, for example traced many of women's psychological problems to penis envy and put forth the notion that without castration anxiety, girls could not possibly develop an adequate conscience. When Karen Horney suggested that perhaps boys and men envied women's wombs, she was soundly ridiculed (by some of my own professors) even though the rest of her work was highly respected.[7]

A classic piece of research entitled "Sex Role Stereotypes and clinical Judgments of Mental Health,"[8] investigated the judgments of clinicians (psychiatrists, clinical psychologists and social workers) on criteria of mental health for males and females. One third of the clinicians were asked to indicate the personality characteristics that would describe a mature, healthy male; one third were asked to do this for a mature healthy female; and one third were asked to do this for a mature healthy adult. There were no significant differences between the standards for males and for adults. There were, however differences between the standards for females and for adults. The standards of mental health for women would have been considered unhealthy for "adults" or for men. Another result of the study was that socially desirable characteristics were likely to be assigned to males and undesirable ones to females. So ingrained and unconscious are these stereotypes that the results were true of female as well as male clinicians. The most destructive aspect of this picture is that women internalize the message that we are weak and inferior and that our very bodies are "lacking" an important appendage.

Think about those thousands of years when God was a woman and women were revered. They constitute the longest span of our human heritage. As women we need to know that for most of our time on Earth human beings considered the female body to be sacred and conceived of the Divine in female form. That image of the Great Goddess affirms our female bodies as sacred. For millennia the Goddess was, in Joseph Campbell's words "a metaphysical symbol: the arch personification of the power of Space, Time and Matter, within whose bounds all beings arise and die..And everything having form or name...was Her child within Her womb."[9] "There can be no doubt that in the very earliest ages of human history the magical force and wonder of the female was no less a marvel than the universe itself and this gave to women a prodigious power."[10]

Perhaps we should look into our mirrors again. Let us see ourselves this time as the sacred creators and preservers of life. Our distinctive shapes and curves, the colors and textures of our hair, as wonderful as they are varied, and all beautiful. Let us exclaim with poet Ntosake Shange "I found God within myself, and I loved Her. I loved Her fiercely!"[11]

TWO

Reclaiming
Our Sexuality

LIGHT YOUR SPECIAL CANDLE and place beside it your favorite scented oil, perfume or body lotion. Think about your most beautiful and sacred sexual self. Run your hands gently over the contours of your body; feel its unique curves and angles. Caress the softness of your hair, the smoothness of your face. Lightly massage your arms or legs. Be aware of the pleasures of touch. Hug yourself. Think of the best, the most deeply satisfying lover you have ever had. Feel the warmth, the excitement, the passionate physical attraction you shared. Breathe deeply and allow yourself to be fully in touch with the joy of your sexual life.

Take a few moments now to ponder these questions. How do you feel about your sexual experiences? Have you found great pleasure and joy there? Have you perhaps found pain and disappointment? What do you like least about love-making? What do you enjoy most? Write down your responses in your journal.

As modern women we live in a society which buys, sells, distorts, demeans and degrades female sexuality in films, on TV, in literature, in humor, and most visibly in advertising. In our cultural efforts to break out of the Puritan and Victorian repression of sexuality we have reduced the beauty and wholeness of woman to an object to be displayed, an image to be used to sell everything from magazines to cigarettes to cars to airline travel. Our sexual revolution has failed to liberate women because it has not addressed the deeper problem which pre-dates and helped to reinforce the repressions of the Puritan and Victorian ages. That deeper problem is the driving need that patriarchal societies have to control and limit the power of female sexuality. Whether that control is accomplished by repression, by teaching women that sex is something to be endured rather than enjoyed, by commercial and personal exploitation, or by teaching women that being sexy is something they must do to please men, the result for women is the same. Not only are women's sexual desires and needs not considered; our very bodies are subject to control, manipulation and mutilation by men and their laws. We need to ask why, and we need to take a long look at human history to find the answer.

Let us journey back into the mists of pre-history and ask just what it was that enabled our species to become human. According to Monica Sjoo and Barbara Mor what made our species human in the very beginning was a series of evolutionary changes that occurred in the female body.[1] These changes were: the elimination of the estrus cycle and the development of the menstrual cycle which meant that women were capable of sexual activity at any time; the development of the clitoris and evolution of the vagina which meant greatly enhanced sexuality and orgasmic potential; a change from rear to frontal sex which resulted in a prolonged and enhanced lovemaking period and the personalization of sex, and; the development of breasts which added to woman's potential for sexual arousal. Because of these radical changes in the female body, human beings became the only creatures on earth for whom copulation occurs for nonreproductive purposes: for pleasure, for social bonding, for shelter and comfort. Notice that these changes were not primarily related to reproduction but to human sexual relationship.

The entire development of human culture was initiated by these changes in the human female body. Scholars have known for some time that it was from the first inner circle of women—the cave, the first hearth, the place of birth—that human society evolved. The use of symbols for speech, for marking time, for painting and sculpting images, and the development of agriculture all originated with the women. The effects of dramatic changes in the human female body, however, have barely been mentioned.

Take a few moments now to absorb the immensity of the fact that all of human culture was initiated by the evolutionary advance which was the human female menstrual cycle. *"We were not human until the appearance of the menstrual cycle."*[2] Think about that. Think about the sacredness of your female sexuality.

Quite naturally then, it was the female body which was central in the very earliest human spiritual or religious expression. Archeologist G. Rachel Levy has carefully documented the fact that the first 30,000 years of human existence revolved around the celebration of female processes.[3] A great cosmic analogy was made between the mysteries of menstruation, pregnancy and childbirth and the abundance of the Earth and its cycles of time. The more recent archeological work of Marija Gimbutas confirms these ideas and reinforces the startling suggestion that the first "God" we knew as human beings was female.[4] Early Stone Age people, in Levy's words "bequeathed to all humanity a foundation of ideas upon which the mind could raise its structures."[5]

Sjoo and Mor list some of these primal ideas and images: "The cave as the female womb; the mother as a pregnant Earth; the magical fertile female as the mother of all animals; the Venus of Laussel standing with the horn of the moon upraised in her hand; the cave as the female tomb where life is buried, painted blood red, and awaiting rebirth."[6]

Let us look now at the attitudes toward female sexuality in our own times. An Egyptian woman came to me for counseling a few years ago. She had married an American serviceman and had come with him to this country. She was becoming more and more concerned that her husband might lose interest in her because she was unable to enjoy sexual intercourse. She finally revealed that she had been given a clitoridectomy as a young girl. This surgery amputates the clitoris; it severs the nerves needed for orgasm. Some cultures even today brutally, physically rob women of the pleasure of their sexuality. In 1976 an estimated 10 million women were subjected to this operation.[7] The practice continues unabated in many Islamic and African tribal societies.

Former Vice President Dan Quayle appeared on TV in 1988 answering a young girl's question about abortion by coldly stating that even if a young woman was raped she should not be allowed to terminate the pregnancy but should be forced to bear an unwanted child. Thus has our own culture in our own times attempted to rob women of control over their own bodies. Whether or not we as individuals would choose an abortion it seems to me that the choice should be ours as women.

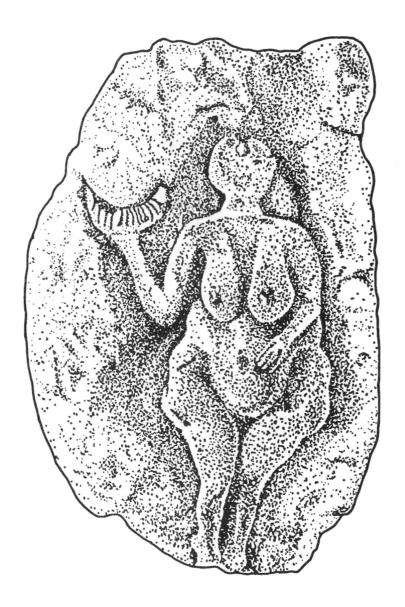

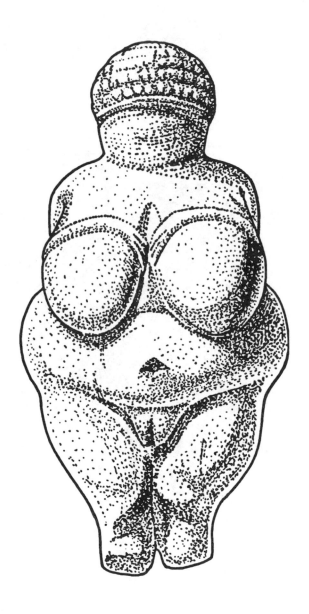

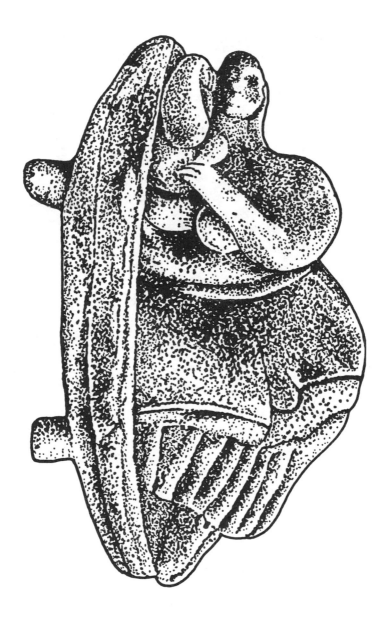

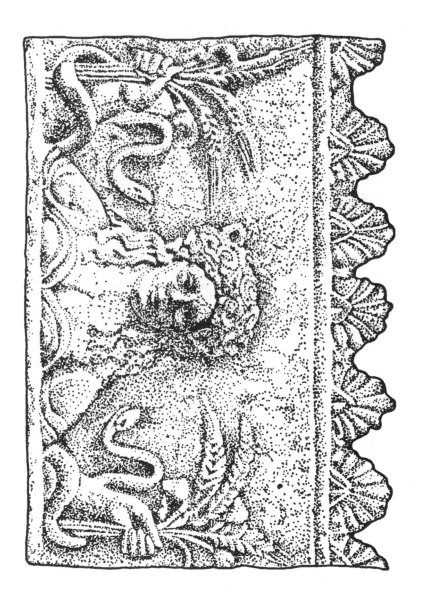

The rape of women has always been an unspoken part of the spoils of patriarchal war. More recently it was used openly and deliberately as a weapon against the women of Bosnia. Thus do so-called civilized nations use the bodies of women to further their territorial plans.

One of the most stubbornly ignored biological discoveries of our time is that all mammalian embryos, male and female, are anatomically female during the early stages of fetal life. Stephen Jay Gould writes, "The female course of development is, in a sense, biologically intrinsic to all mammals...The male route is a modification induced by secretions of androgens from the developing testes."[8] Males, it seems, are derived from the primary female pattern. Men of course have not wanted to know this basic biological fact. They did not discover it until 1951 and then proceeded to ignore it until a woman scientist, Mary Jane Sherfey brought it to light again in 1961.[9]

A related and equally disturbing (to men) fact about embryos is that the clitoris and the penis develop from the same precursor. As Sjoo and Mor put it "Women are used to hearing the clitoris described as an `undeveloped penis;' men are not used to thinking of the penis as an overdeveloped clitoris."[10] The clitoris is in fact the only organ meant exclusively for erotic stimulation; it allows women to separate sexuality from reproduction. Men, in whom the penis carries both semen and sexual response, have repeatedly hypothesized the existence of a vaginal orgasm in women, ignoring or denying the reality of clitoral eroticism. A woman's clitoris is a source of erotic pleasure and orgasm throughout her life, something she can enjoy with or without the help of a male partner. Many women who do not want children or have already raised their families prefer a female partner. That fact does not please patriarchal men who wish to see themselves as in complete control of women's bodies and sexuality.

So ingrained and automatic is the denial and repudiation of the female body in our culture that truly absurd things can happen. Rockefeller University launched a research project on the impact of obesity on breast and uterine cancer and for the first few weeks they studied only men![11] Less obvious but indicative of the same cultural bias, the much heralded research finding that taking one aspirin every other day would lower the risk of heart attack was based upon a study of 22,000 physicians, all men, not one woman included.[12]

When it comes to research money, significantly less is spent on diseases affecting women than on diseases affecting men. In 1987 only 13.5% of National Institutes of Health $6 billion research budget was devoted to diseases unique to or more serious among women.[13] In 1991 the National Institutes of Health spent $800 million on AIDS research and only $92.7 million on breast cancer research, even though breast cancer kills almost twice as many women each year, about 46,000, compared to all AIDS deaths—about 24,000 people a year.[14] We do not begrudge the money spent for something as important as AIDS research, but we need to ask why the priorities are such that women always come last. In *Megatrends for Women*, Patricia Aburdeen and John Naisbitt report that breast cancer strikes one in nine American women. The authors then tell the following story:

> "In October 1991, 3000 women marched to Boston's City Hall to hear speakers call for more research and better treatment for breast cancer. When *The Boston Globe* covered the rally with a photograph and no story, dozens of angry women called the paper's ombudsman. Said one woman, `If one man in nine lost a testicle, it would be on page one!'"[15]

Medical treatment has also discriminated against women especially in the case of heart disease. When men and women present similar symptoms men are twice as likely to have adequate diagnostic testing and twice as likely to be given by-pass surgery, angioplasty (a balloon-like device is used to unclog arteries) or "clot busters" which stop heart attacks in progress.[16] There is in fact no research data on whether or not such treatment would be effective on women. But evidence of the lack of "aggressive" treatment clearly suggests that women are not now being appropriately treated for heart attacks.

These demands by women for more "aggressive" medical treatment may sound somewhat strange to women who have studied even minimally the deadly history of male medicine's effects upon women. Men may not treat our hearts aggressively but they have gone far beyond aggressive in the treatment of our sexual parts.

As male physicians replaced female midwives in Europe more and more women died in childbirth, victims of infections spread by the male doctors who went from autopsy and disease to childbirth without bothering to wash their hands. Mary Daly chronicles the horrors of American gynecology including the infamous operations of J. Marion Sims. He performed sexual operations, first on black female slaves, later on indigent women at the Woman's Hospital in New York. Daly reports that "Mary Smith, an Irish indigent, suffered thirty of his operations between 1856 and 1859. The black slave Anarcha had suffered the same number in his backyard stable a decade before."[17] Sims was hailed as one of our most distinguished gynecologists. Clitoridectomy was promoted as a cure for masturbation, and removal of the ovaries as a cure for "insanity." For several decades ovariotomy was an extremely popular "cure" for "unacceptable" behavior in women.

In the 20th century complete hysterectomies and radical mastectomies became the order of the day, the latter now known to be mostly unnecessary. In the area of contraception the painful side effects of the IUD and the Pill are legendary, enshrined in the folk music of our times by such songs as Judy Small's poignant reversal called "The IPD" (Intra Penile Device). In the chorus she sings, "And when the pain begins to fill your eyes with tears, remember, I put up with it for years."[18]   Most recently we have seen women persuaded to undergo operations to increase the size of their breasts with silicone implants, implants that sometimes leak and cause multiple health problems.

While we organize to demand the best in medical care, we need to remain aware of the atrocious track record of the patriarchal medical establishment in its treatment of women, especially women's sexual organs.

Undergirding and reinforcing these obvious abuses is a longstanding religious and philosophical attitude that our bodies, especially our female sexual bodies are unclean, obscene and evil. The early philosophers of Christianity are notorious for their negative attitudes toward sexuality.[19] St. Jerome ordered "Regard everything as poison which bears within it the seed of sensual pleasure." Tertullian declared that the sex act rendered even marriage obscene. St. Augustine said that sexual intercourse is never sinless, even within marriage. And in the First Letter of John in the Bible we are told "Love not the world, neither things that are in the world...for all that is in the world, the lust of the flesh, and the lust of the eyes, and the pride of life, is not of the Father."

On the subject of women's bodies the Church Fathers had even worse things to say. St. Thomas Aquinas insisted "that every woman is birth-defective, an imperfect male begotten because her father happened to be ill, weakened, or in a state of sin at the time of her conception." St. Odo of Cluny said of woman "How should we desire to embrace what is no more than a sack of dung!" Clement of Alexandria said that "Every woman ought to be filled with shame at the thought that she is a woman."

Through the centuries churchmen perpetuated these attitudes. According to a nineteenth century Anglican churchman women are "intrinsically inferior in excellence, imbecile by sex and nature, weak in body, inconstant in mind, and imperfect and infirm in character." The president of a leading theological school declared "My Bible commands the subjection of women forever." As late as 1971 an Episcopalian bishop said "The sexuality of Christ is no accident nor is his masculinity incidental. This is the divine choice."

Perhaps the writer of the First Letter of John was correct in saying that the lust of the flesh and the lust of the eyes and the pride of life are "not of the Father." Perhaps they are "of the Mother." The Mother who was our very first "God" as human beings.

Our earliest religious images are of the magical pregnant Goddess, and the original transformation mystery is the primordial experience of birth. It is interesting that men's original rituals all over the world were imitations of the female mysteries of menstruation and childbirth. Only in later neolithic times do we find statues of the Goddess shown nursing a male child. One of the earliest shows the Goddess as two female bodies back to back, one embracing a lover, the other nursing an infant. Here we can see the beginning of the worship of the Goddess' son/lover. As human beings became aware of the male's part in conception, the act of coupling, of lovemaking, was also perceived as a sacred part of the continuity of life. Down through the centuries a ritual of sacred mating was performed throughout the ancient world.

Among the Sumerians the Goddess was widely known as Inanna. In Her temples the priestesses were considered sacred representatives of the Goddess. They made love to those who came to pray, so that they would understand the miracle of life through communion with the holiest of women.

Each year a priestess of Inanna performed a sacred mating ritual. She chose for her partner a new young man who would then be appointed Shepherd for the year. He was especially chosen and was called Damuzi, beloved of the Goddess. The priestess, representing the Goddess, bathed and dressed and placed kohl upon her eyes. The new Damuzi came bringing gifts and offerings for the Goddess, and promising to follow the ancient rituals of Inanna. When the congregation gathered, the priestess declared that Damuzi must prove himself upon her bed, give pleasure to her, and she to him. Only then would she appoint him to be the Shepherd of the land.

A bed was set for the priestess and Damuzi. The priestess led the new Damuzi to her bed and assured him of her pleasure in his gifts and offerings and in his beauty. She promised that her love would be more sweet than honey and that she would bless him with the honor of stewardship. This sacred ritual was so much a part of Sumerian life from the earliest of times that later kings called themselves Damuzi, the beloved of Inanna, and believed that they were especially chosen for Her holy lap.[20]

Male historians, learning of such rites have labeled the practice "prostitution," but the word reflects their patriarchal bias rather than the original meaning of the ritual. Women in ancient Goddess-worshipping societies were free to take as many lovers as they chose. Priestesses were called virgins which meant not married or "one-in-herself." The term "virgin" did not refer to sexual chastity but to sexual independence. Temple love-making was not a service to men and no woman performed these rites in order to make a living or by coercion. The ritual was a way for both women and men to participate in the essence of the divine. They believed that the Goddess came into being in that moment of sexual and psychic union.[21]

Return now to your own sexual experiences. Do you feel a real sense of independence about your sexuality? Are you free to love whom you will? How do you feel about the idea of such independence? How do you feel about the idea of sexual union as a moment of Divine presence? In the Charge of the Goddess, a common prayer of invocation, the Goddess declares, "All acts of love and pleasure are my rituals." Imagine a world where pleasure is considered sacred and pleasing to Divinity. Take some time to write down your thoughts and feelings.

Caress and anoint yourself with your favorite lotion or perfume or oil. Know that for millennia the menstrual, life-giving and life-taking female body was worshipped as Divine, and that lovemaking was a sacred ritual. Say aloud: The Goddess affirms my sexual pleasure.

THREE

Reclaiming
Our Power as Women

LIGHT YOUR CANDLE and say aloud: The Goddess is a symbol of female strength and power. The Goddess is a symbol of all that is beautiful in the female experience. The Goddess is a symbol of woman's fierce new love of the Divine in ourselves.

Now do the following exercise. Draw a circle. Divide it into four quarters. In each quarter write a word that describes a feeling you have about power. Choose one of the four words and, under the circle, write a sentence or two about that feeling.

Women who do this exercise almost always write *fear* in one quarter, and fear is the feeling most often chosen as the one to expand into a sentence. Did that happen to you? Even when women have positive feelings about power, the feelings are often accompanied by ambivalence and a tendency to apologize for or rationalize such positive feelings. In discussions the fear and ambivalence is usually related to our definitions of power. Is power strength? Does it mean dominating or controlling others? Can we be both loving and powerful? What are your feelings about power? How would you define power?

One of the most important tasks facing women today is the development of a sense of competence and power. For almost 5,000 years our nature has been defined and circumscribed by men. Only recently have we begun to speak for ourselves and to demand the right to exercise our natural power and competence.

To develop our sense of power we need to understand the ways in which our society and its beliefs and myths tend to reinforce an unequal power relationship between men and women. A common anthropological theory is that the myths of a culture reflect its social power arrangements. If the overarching myth is that of a father-god whose Earthly representative is a man, as in Judaism, Islam and Christianity, this mythology reflects a male-dominated society. Once such a myth is revered in the society, it reinforces the social arrangements as part of the Divine plan. As Mary Daly wrote: "If God in 'his' heaven is a father ruling 'his' people then it is in the 'nature' of things and according to divine plan and the order of the universe that society be male-dominated."[1]

Just think for a moment about our own government. I began to write this in the so-called "Year of the Woman" when we were still looking mostly at men running for the highest offices. With great fanfare we announced a dramatic increase in the number of women elected to the U. S. Senate—from two to six. Sisters, we are more than half the population! We should have at least 51 women senators! We find it thrilling that First Lady Hillary Rodham Clinton, has a real career of her own. One can only wonder why such a woman couldn't run for President herself. Perhaps she didn't want the job but where are the women candidates who do aspire to be President? Running on obscure third party tickets and receiving almost no media attention. Because the major parties "know" that a woman could never win the election. Because in the mythic popular imagination, power still resides in the fathers and sons, with the mothers and daughters as window dressing.

If we look at our personal lives we experience the same kind of assumptions. Take the question of our names. Who are you? Whose name do you carry? Your father's or your husband's? We have had the power of our names stolen from us. We may have first or middle names that are the same as those of our female ancestors but for all official purposes we are known by our family names, that is, the names of our fathers or husbands. Does it really help to retain your father's name when you get married?

The loss of our names is like the loss of our own identities. Indeed, for many centuries and until only recently a married woman was subsumed into the identity of her husband. As recently as the 1970s a woman colleague of mine, a psychologist who was married, tried to get an oil company credit card in her own name, separate from that of her husband so she could more easily keep track of her own car expenses. She was employed full-time and had an ample income but she refused to give her husband's name on the application so the oil company turned down her request. She fought the decision and eventually was given her own account. But the old assumption was that her husband should be the responsible cardholder, that she existed only as part of him despite her professional status and employment. Many women thought they had their own credit cards until they were divorced. They discovered then that the accounts could be closed by their ex-husbands who were well aware that they, not their wives, had the final power over the accounts. It made no difference whether the family income was provided by the husband or the wife or both. Everything was issued in his name and that gave him the final power.

Some of these practices have been changed but the old assumptions die hard. Just this year I visited my daughter, Laura, in order to meet the parents of her fiance. I told her to make a reservation at a nice restaurant and I would take the five of us out to dinner. It would be my treat. We had a pleasant dinner but when the check came the waitress automatically put it down in front of the older man, the father of Laura's fiance. He looked embarrassed and I had to reach awkwardly for the check. Of course the waitress didn't know they were my guests, but instead of asking she made an old assumption.

Money figures strongly in any analysis of power in our society because we tend to use money as a measure of value and importance. For me the clearest indication of the position of women in relation to money was the question we were often asked when we were young mothers: "Do you work?" The questioner usually meant "Do you work outside the home?" Whatever we did at home in the way of housework or caring for our children was assumed to be "doing nothing." No monetary value was placed on that activity. No monetary value is placed on it even today and the question "Do you work?" is still asked of young mothers. In a society that measures value in terms of money the meaning is very clear. Homemaking, the care and nurturing of our children just doesn't count as real work. Outside the home professions and jobs which women have been able to enter in great numbers tend to be poorly paid. Even today in the wake of the feminist movement we are learning about the "glass ceiling," the invisible, unspoken, but very real barriers that keep women out of the most prestigious and highest paying jobs.

Perhaps the most destructive way in which our culture limits the power of women is by socializing us to believe within our own hearts that we are less strong, less worthy, less intelligent than men. I don't believe that in my head but sometimes in my heart I still do. A male colleague, a minister, routinely takes wealthy male church members out to lunch to encourage their generous gifts to the church. Whenever I think of all the old habits and assumptions I would have to overcome in order to do that, I quake. As a woman I still find it difficult to call a man, invite him to lunch, discuss church finances and pick up the check. When I ask myself why it is difficult, it comes down to the old assumption that the man, especially a wealthy successful man, is more important than I, that his time is more valuable than mine, that I am not on an equal footing with him. "Who do I think I am anyway?" I ask myself in these moments of crippling doubt. I have to work very hard every day to put those old doubts behind me and that work robs me of vital energy, the power I need to do my job well.

Even if we break the old habits we may yet fear the meaning of power. As women we are carefully taught to be caring, to put the needs of others ahead of our own. Often we convince ourselves that our needs are identical to those of our fathers or husbands or children. If we claim our own strength, assert our own needs as valid and distinct from the needs of others, won't we be seen as unloving, uncaring? We may not want to abandon the high value we place on love and caring for others. Yet we want to develop our own talents, assert our own needs. How can we do both?

In *Toward a New Psychology of Women,* Jean Baker Miller makes an important distinction between power *for* ourselves and power *over* others.[2] Our male-dominated society has tended to define power as power over others, the ability to control. Someone else's power, then, is seen as dangerous because he or she will want to control you. Miller points out that in terms of human development this is not a valid or healthy definition of power. Real confidence in oneself and real power for oneself have the opposite effect—they reduce the need to have power over others or to control them. It is important for women to hold fast to this healthy definition of power and to understand that we do not need to diminish other women, or men, in order to assert our own strength.

It is important for women to understand that ancient myths and artifacts emphasized female power for thousands of years, thus reflecting female power in social structures. When women today assert themselves and regain significant power, our myths will begin to reflect that shift.

In the days of Sumer, the chief deity was female and the chief clergy were women. In the ancient world the Goddess was known by many names, as was her consort. Each Sumerian city had a Goddess or a God of a different name as its special deity. It has been very important to me as a woman to know that the female chief deity was powerful as well as nurturing, and that her priestesses were real women acknowledged in their society for their wisdom and influence. Consider Enheduanna, a real woman, a high priestess, poet, and thealogian who lived about 2,360 B.C.E. in the Sumerian city of Ur. She knew the Goddess as Inanna.

In order to unite several city states, Enheduanna wrote a series of hymns to Inanna ascribing many marvelous attributes to the Goddess and insisting that She was greater than any other deity. Her hope was that if she could unite the people in worshipping the same deity, she could then more easily unite them politically. In her poetic work "The Exaltation of Inanna" ("Nin-Me-Sar-Ra"), Enheduanna wrote: "Lady who soothes the rains, Lady who gladdens the heart, whose rage is not tempered, Oh Lady supreme over the land, who has ever denied you homage?"[3] In these hymns, Inanna not only soothes the rains and gladdens the heart; She also rages, has a terrible glance, is lofty as heaven and broad as the Earth. *She has power!*

Excavations at Ur show that in later times, many centuries after Enheduanna lived and wrote there, a Moon Goddess reigned as the partner of the Moon God. From the excavation of the royal tombs of Ur came beautifully constructed lyres. The oldest music in the world has come down to us on clay tablets; it is a Hurrian hymn to the moon Goddess, dated to about 1400 B.C.E. Both instrumental and vocal music played a great role in Sumerian life, and some musicians became important in both temple and court. One elaborately decorated lyre was carved with the bull's head, a symbol of the Goddess' beloved son and consort, a symbol we will encounter again as we explore the ancient religion of the Goddess.

The excavation at Mari, another Sumerian city-state, has given especially strong support to the theory that where the Goddess reigned, women had significant political and social power. Scholars grudgingly admit that in Mari women served as governors. In ancient times, when the Goddess reigned, both women and men dedicated themselves to her service. Her temples were the creative centers of ancient societies, centers of wisdom and law, of commerce where all the accounts were kept, centers for understanding sexuality and human relationships, centers of agricultural knowledge and fertility, of music, art, dance, and of every aspect of human existence.

Take a few moments now to reflect upon your own life experience. With your candle burning, ask yourself two questions: What difference would it have made in your personal life if the god of this culture had been spoken of as female when you were growing up? What difference would it have made in the power structures of our society? Meditate now on your worth as a person, your special talents and abilities, your achievements and your most daring goals. What is your heart's desire? Look at the candle flame and be in touch with your personal passion and energy. Know in your heart that you can be powerful as well as loving, that your strength will not diminish others but will empower them. Know that you are a person of worth and competence, and dare to be so!

Where the Goddess was worshipped Her temples were the centers of wisdom, culture, and financial power, presided over by women. Remember that. The Goddess affirms female power.

FOUR

Reclaiming
the Power of Money

LIGHT YOUR SPECIAL CANDLE and place a few coins beside it. Read the following meditation:

How much time do you spend thinking about money? Where will your next money come from? How will you spend that money? What is more important to you than money? What is money?

Money is completely worthless; yet it is universally treasured. Love of money is said to be the root of all evil; yet the pursuit of money is our one common purpose. Money is completely impersonal; yet it makes possible our own personhood. Money enslaves us; yet it sets us free.

Money is no measure of real worth; yet it is our only common standard of value. Money is morally neutral; yet it contaminates and corrupts. Money is given and received; yet it is never a gift. Money is unreal; yet it defines reality. Money is a power that possesses us; yet we can possess its power.

Money is a deity to be respected.

Take some time to write in your journal some of your own feelings about money. Do you think that being a woman affects your attitudes toward money?

Money, like writing, seems to have originated in the temples of the ancient world. The word *money* comes from the Roman Goddess Juno who in one of her forms was called Moneta meaning She Who Gives Warning. Her temple in Rome was the center for the finances of Rome and so her name Moneta became the word money. The same word became also *mint* because that same temple was the place where coins were minted. According to Barbara Walker silver and gold coins manufactured there were valuable not only by reason of their precious metal but also by the blessing of the Goddess herself which was believed to bring good fortune and healing magic.[1]

Money was indeed a magical invention. Folk tales are full of magic lamps and genies and beanstalks, of magical ways to have our every wish granted. We would all like to be able to snap our fingers or twitch our noses and have our purposes accomplished. And that is almost exactly what happens with money. It can be exchanged for every conceivable kind of real wealth. Magic. Pure magic. So enamored were people of this magical invention that it became over time the primary measure of real wealth in Western society.

Why then do three quite diverse philosophical or intellectual traditions agree on the idea that money is somehow unclean or something to be despised?

One of those traditions is Christianity. About one third of the parables of Jesus are about money. He is reported to have taught that being rich is a barrier to salvation and to have told the rich young man to sell everything and give his money to the poor. The one time he is depicted as angry is when he turns over the tables of the money changers at the temple. His advice on taxes is to render unto Caesar what is Caesar's, to separate money and worldly concerns from one's religion. Classical Christianity has preached, if not practiced, that money and this world are to be renounced in favor of an other-worldly kingdom of heaven. The love of money, said St. Paul, is the root of all evil.

Classical Marxism also renounces money as responsible for the alienation of human beings from their labor. People no longer work to create or produce, but only to make money. This situation Marx considered to be disastrous. He felt it was labor which was of essential value and that all monetary valuations were to be discarded. Those who seek only money he saw as exploiting those who work.

Finally there is Freud who thought money was anal. He equated money with feces, excrement. It is therefore filthy and messy. Withholding money is a kind of constipation. Money is related to the bowels and is dirty. And indeed, we do refer to money sometimes as "filthy lucre."

Christianity, Marxism and Freudianism all agree on despising money. As a psychologist I have learned to pay careful attention to those things another person protests most vehemently against. And as a woman I have learned to pay close attention to those things which our great patriarchs preach most loudly against. Because, of course, what is loudly despised is often what is covertly desired or feared or worshipped. So if Jesus, Marx and Freud are all in agreement on something, we women had better take a careful look.

Women are socialized to live out the Christian ideals of self-sacrifice and martyrdom and men are socialized to give lip service to them. The same hypocrisy would seem to apply to what is preached about money. Filthy, despicable, and barrier to salvation it may be, but the fact is that in general, men have money and women don't. According to the United Nations Labor Organization, women put in 65% of the world's work and get back only 10% of all income paid. The female half of the world's population owns less than 1% of world property.[2] Women in our Western society may have access to money through their husbands or fathers, but until recently women rarely accumulated or controlled their own large fortunes.

Men may philosophize about the distinction between money, which is "merely" a measure, and "real wealth," the goods and services into which money can be changed. They can say that the pursuit of money leads to an unhappy, hollow existence. They can urge upon women the virtues of simplicity. But for most men the ultimate appeal is to the "bottom line," that is, to money. How much money will something cost? How much financial profit will be gleaned? Mae West cut through this hypocrisy with great clarity when she said "I've been rich and I've been poor, and rich is better."

In his fascinating book *The Seven Laws of Money* Michael Phillips suggests that the seventh law is that there are worlds without money.[3] When you are asleep and dreaming, that's a world without money, and there may be other places in the universe and other states of life in which there is no money. The point is that in this world, our world, everything we do is related to money.

Our architecture and our language are very revealing. A hundred years ago the tallest most impressive buildings in a city were the churches. Today the churches are dwarfed by banks and insurance companies. One of the most popular Christmas cards sold every year in New York City shows the church at the head of Wall Street surrounded by the much taller towers of finance. And if you visit Salt Lake City you can go to the top of the Mormon Church-owned office building and look down on the famous temple across the street. The architecture of a bank is supposed to function for us like that of a temple. It conveys strength, power and security in ways that churches no longer do.

Our language is even more revealing. A few years ago during a cross-country move I stopped in Denver to visit my friend Ann. In one of our conversations she was speaking with great enthusiasm about the financial rewards of her work as a real estate broker. Suddenly she stopped, gave me a piercing look and asked, "Shirley, do you know your net worth?" I knew she meant financial net worth and I pointed to my car and the U-Haul truck parked in her driveway. But I was struck by the many levels of meaning involved in the words we use about money. Consider the names we use for banks: trust, security, mutual, first, saving.

Banks have been called the centers of our society, places of security where we save our money and store our valuable possessions. We go to banks to seek help, to borrow, to receive credit. Our worth is measured by our credit rating determined by banks. The word *credit* comes from the same root as the word creed and it means faith, belief. Banks are involved in all the transitions of life. A child's first step toward autonomy is often the opening of a bank account. We become adults when we have a checking account. Marriages begin with a joint bank account. Homes are bought with bank approved mortgages. New businesses are financed by banks. Organizations need bank accounts and as officers change the bank must be notified. In short, the centers of money are the centers of power, power which affects every aspect of our lives.

As women in our culture have gained access to more and more financial resources, however, another commercial-financial institution has appeared—the shopping mall. Malls may be owned and operated by men but they are built primarily to meet the needs of women shoppers. Unlike the older banks, malls are often not tall and impressive but sprawling and circular. Whereas banks have only money, malls have the goods and services into which the magical money can be changed. There are shops of all sizes selling just about everything one could want for personal or home use. There are restaurants for lunch and coffee shops where one can rest one's feet and sip a hot or cold drink. There are toy stores, video games, record stores and sports shops for the children and teens. One mall I know of even has a huge carousel in the center. In cold or very hot climates the entire complex is enclosed and heated or air-conditioned. In some parts of California the malls are open air with outdoor cafes and colorful gardens.

Elite philosophers will say that malls are mind-numbing purveyors of commercialism and certainly there is much truth in that assessment. But once again I hear the hypocrisy of a message aimed at women, namely that we should be "less materialistic." I would answer that women have been the ones responsible for the material needs of their families. In most families even today no one else is going to see that there are towels in the bathroom, curtains at the windows or shoes on the children's feet. I mean the actual physical activity of going to the mall and acquiring the needed items. As every woman who manages a household knows, there are always needed items. She may be using her husband's earnings, her own earnings or a combination of both but she is almost always the one who is responsible for the household budget and the shopping.

I think of my friend Chris whom I met when she was a middle-aged graduate student. The last of her six children had just left to be on her own and Chris had moved into student housing. The apartment she shared with other students had no kitchen and the students took their meals in a big dining hall. I saw Chris right after she had eaten her first meal there. She said "You know it was the most amazing experience. Here was all this food and all I had to do was just put it on my plate and eat." She paused, tears came into her eyes and she said "This is the first time in 31 years that I haven't been responsible for someone else's food." She explained that of course, her children had all learned to fix meals and often did so, but that Mom was the one who saw to it that there was food there to be cooked. And I would add, apropos of malls, clothes to be worn and all sorts of household equipment to be used. Other students often complained about the dining hall food. Not Chris. She continued to perceive it as an amazing adventure, one that freed her to do the serious intellectual work she had been longing to do.

As a young woman I resisted the idea of having to choose between a professional career and a family. I felt it was an unfair choice. I wanted "the whole thing." My husband, like some others, used to say "I help my wife with the shopping (or dishes or cleaning)." I felt fortunate to have his help. It was many years before I heard the subliminal message in his words which was that I, as wife, was still the one responsible for such chores. Make no mistake about it; shopping is a chore. But I quickly discovered that a trip to the mall could also ease the chronic malaise that goes along with living a stereotyped role and not knowing what is wrong. (The "problem that has no name" as Betty Friedan called it.)

As a woman I became very aware that malls are not just for shopping, even though the banks now often have automatic tellers or small branch offices within the malls. No, malls are for dreaming, for escaping, for turning the kids loose so you can sit down with a magazine and a soothing cup of tea. Malls can distract us from the painful truths of our lives. I used to buy myself a new blouse or some scented soap and go home feeling a little better. Later, as I journeyed further into myself and away from the expectations of others I still went to the mall. On most of my trips there I bought nothing—except perhaps for a cup of coffee or a scoop of frozen yogurt. I still like to sit there with my coffee, reading feminist books, writing letters or even serious papers, with the vibrant energy of women and children swirling around me. Maybe it just serves to remind me of the long journey we have to make as women in order to be free. I feel comfortable there. I would not feel comfortable doing that in a bank.

How do you feel about malls? How do you feel about banks?

As women we need to remember that the Goddess temples of the ancient world, the centers of financial power, were presided over by women. The financial institutions of our society today, be they banks or malls, are presided over by men.

According to Patricia Aburdeen and John Naisbitt if you scan the 1992 Fortune 500 list of companies you will find only one woman chief executive officer.[4] A 1991 report by the Feminist Majority Foundation found that in these same Fortune 500 companies there were 6,502 corporate officers at the level of vice president or above and only 175 were women. Women also earn consistently less than men—in 1991, 74 cents for every dollar men earn. Women executives are sometimes considered bargains. Companies realize they save 25 to 30 per cent by hiring women.

Money is a marvelous invention. In and of itself it is morally neutral. Like power of any kind, however, it becomes dangerous when cut off from an ethic of justice and caring. Perhaps the worst advice Jesus ever uttered was to render unto Caesar what is Caesar's and to God what is God's, that is, to separate the power of money from the love of justice and compassion.

A classic modern example of this separation is the so-called development of Third World countries. Family agriculture which could sustain the population was abandoned in order to develop cash crops which could be sold to other countries. The cash crops made a few men wealthy but impoverished the rest of the population, and in many places destroyed or depleted precious natural resources. In the U.S. we see this separation of money from ethics resulting in the use of profits to pay excessive dividends or executive salaries rather than for the research and development of improved products and services, or for worker safety and environmental concerns. Whenever there is a choice between shareholder's profits and environmental safety, the Earth and all her plants and creatures are usually the losers—even when those plants and creatures are children in a place like Love Canal.

In our personal lives the same split between justice and the power of money can result in the use of money to control the behavior of people who are financially dependent, namely women. If a mother chooses to stay at home while her children are young she is financially dependent upon her husband. That situation gives him tremendous power in the relationship. Whether or not he discusses financial decisions with her, the hard fact is that the pay checks are made out to him and he can, if he wants, demand his own way. If a woman objects to her husband's financial control she may suffer the loss of the relationship and she will have to face the reality that it is still very difficult for a single mother to earn enough money to support herself and pay for child care. Nor would it be wise for her to count on receiving child support from an ex-husband as only a very small percentage of men ever actually pay it. If the power of money were relinked to justice, perhaps our society would be restructured so that no woman, nor any man, would have to be financially dependent in order to care for children.

As women, let us claim our right to a fair share of the world's money and to the power that money can give us. But let us strive to build a society in which that power will be used in ways that will enhance the quality of life for ourselves and our children and our planet. As an old bumper sticker said: It will be a great day when schools have plenty of money and the Air Force has to hold a bake sale to build a bomber.

Return now to your own feelings about money and its place in your life. Do you feel you are adequately paid for the work you do? What great projects do you dream of doing if only you had the money?

The first law of money, according to Phillips is "Do it! Money will come when you are doing the right thing."[5] The "right thing" is the work or project you have a passion to do for its own sake. This law restores the value and dignity of creative work for its own sake without despising money. The idea is that if your project is good enough and you pour your personal energy and time into it and work hard enough the money will follow. Money by itself cannot accomplish your goal. Only you can do it. Phillips' advice is to go ahead and do what you want to do. Worry about your ability to do it but not about the money. If you have enough passion within yourself you will find an almost infinite number of ways to make a living at the things you want to do.

Do you agree with Phillips? Is that first law of money—Do it!—true for women? Can we really find ways to make a living doing what we as women want to do? Write down your feelings and ideas about such a "law."

Aburdeen and Naisbitt seem to suggest that something akin to this first law of money is already happening with women. They point out that more than five million small to medium size businesses today are led by women. They predict that these businesses will become the top companies of the future. And while Fortune 500 companies have been losing jobs, businesses owned by women are creating new jobs every year.[6]

Pick up your coins and consider the place of money in your own life. Know that you can possess some of its magic if you will look within and discover the power of your own passion. The story is told that Oya, the African Yoruba orisha or Goddess of whirlwinds and transformation heard a human crying, "Please, Twirling Woman, help me, help me!" Oya flashed Her dark mirror and said "If you wish release, Human, simply look into my mirror and change. You who need courage...look into my mirror and change. If you desire wisdom, simply...look into my mirror and change. Power can be yours if you will...look into my mirror and change."

And so the human looked into Her mirror and changed![7]

FIVE

Reclaiming
Mother-Daughter Relationships

LIGHT YOUR SPECIAL CANDLE and allow yourself to relax as you gaze into its flame. Then read the following poem by Ellen Bass, *For My Mother:*

I am afraid to begin this poem
I take a walk to the mailbox. I make a cup of tea.
I call opening lines into my head. None have power.
All the poems I've written of Dad, Herb, lovers—
and you, the one person I
    trust to love me, to be there for me,
as long as you live, you, I don't know how to write to.

There is so much I could say to you, so much I feel
    for you,
So intimately my life is bound with yours; my life
    is yours,
this way we go beyond time, this way we are all of
    who we have been, will be, at once.
I think of Anne Sexton's words: "A woman is her

mother. That's the main thing."[1]

Breathe deeply and reflect upon the poet's words. Are you your mother? Call to mind images of your mother, biological or adopted, the woman who was responsible for nurturing and caring for you as you grew up. Was she good to you? Are the images you have of her positive? Was she a negative force in your life? Are the images you have of her painful? Are you like her in any way? Do you resemble her in body or in personality? In what ways are you glad to be like her? In what ways would you rather be different from her? How has your relationship with your mother changed since you became an adult? It can change within yourself even if your mother is no longer living. Take a few moments to ponder that relationship, and to write down your responses.

As women raised in a patriarchal society we have terrible problems in our mother-daughter relationships. As tiny children both girls and boys must gradually separate from their mothers and go out into the world of their fathers. To do this we reject our mothers. In adolescence we have to break away again from all parental authority if we are to become truly adults. The problem for girls in patriarchy is that to be accepted as "feminine" they must never grow up. Instead of establishing their own identities at adolescence they are conditioned to exchange dependence upon their fathers for dependence upon their husbands—to move from being "Daddy's little girl" to husband's "little doll." Our mothers unwittingly participate in this stunting of our growth by encouraging us to fit the societal stereotype of woman: one who makes every effort to please others, especially men, who believes that even her best talents cannot compete with those of a man, who accepts the limited and limiting roles offered her in a patriarchal society. Because we fail to journey into our own depths to find our personal strength we can never then return to our mothers as adults and enjoy a new and satisfying relationship.

In addition, male dominated psychology and sociology have relished the process of blaming mothers for every problem imaginable. Both young men and young women are taught to blame and reject their mothers far more than their fathers.

Even if a daughter receives strong encouragement from her father and the adult male world to develop her talents she still has reason to resent her mother. By living out the traditional role of the patriarchal woman who denies her own talents in deference to those of men, a mother gives her daughter a strong message which may either stunt her growth and cause deep resentment, or cause an achieving daughter to look upon her mother with contempt. Either way our mother-daughter relationships are troubled. As women we are all daughters. Only by becoming fully adult can we return to our mothers with compassion for the roles they felt forced to take, as well as joy in the new roles we ourselves are exploring.

We need to recognize too the blatant unreality of this patriarchal image of woman as weak and inferior. Only a privileged few have been able to afford the luxury of "staying home." Most women have always worked outside the home, albeit for scandalously low wages, and shouldered all the domestic chores of child rearing as well. Sojourner Truth made the point a long time ago.

> "That man over there says that women need to be helped into carriages and lifted over ditches and to have the best place everywhere. Nobody ever helps me into carriages, or over mud-puddles, or gives me any best place!"

"And ain't I a woman? Look at me! Look at my arm!

I have ploughed and planted, and gathered into barns, and no man could head me! And ain't I a woman? I could work as much and eat as much as a man—when I could get it—and bear the lash as well! And ain't I a woman? I have borne thirteen children and seen them most all sold off to slavery, and when I cried out with my mother's grief, none but Jesus heard me! And ain't I a woman?"[2]

Only by first understanding our own strengths can we begin to recognize the very real strength and courage our mothers often had beneath the selfless facade. At their best they loved and nurtured us, comforted and encouraged us, and stood sometimes as a buffer or protection from the cruelties of the world.

Sometimes a mother's behavior gave us messages in opposition to the stereotypes which surrounded us. My mother thought she had to give up her dreams of drama and journalism in order to marry and have a family. No one ever encouraged her to do otherwise. She lived her life as a traditional housewife. She also taught me carefully to write and to speak. When I continued in college and graduate school after I was married and had children she insisted upon typing all my papers. She understood the pressure I was under trying to be the original Supermom who could do it all. She never said anything but I knew she wanted me to succeed. Yet even that positive encouragement carried another message as I came to realize that the time she spent typing my work could have been spent developing her own talents. Many years later a therapist summed it up succinctly when she asked me "Are you trying to live your mother's life as well as your own?" Perhaps so. I have often wept over the waste of my mother's talents. Marge Piercy's words speak powerfully to me:

...Understand:
I am my mother's daughter,
a small woman of large longings...

I am her only novel.
The plot is melodramatic,
hot lovers leap out of
thickets, it makes you cry
a lot, in between the revolutionary
heroics and making good
home-cooked soup.
Understand: I am my mother's
novel daughter: I
have my duty to perform.[3]

Whatever form our personal journey may take it is crucial to our wholeness as women, as mothers and daughters, that we risk that adventure. The mystery religion which developed around the myth of Demeter and Persephone had such a powerful impact on people that the rites were celebrated for over 2000 years. Try to grasp the immensity of the fact that the chief Divine actors in this drama were a mother and her daughter. Not a father and his son as in the religious mythology of our own culture.

The Myth of Demeter and Persephone

The Goddess Demeter and Her lovely Daughter, Persephone, watched over the plants and the crops that fed the humans entrusted to their care. Demeter had taught the mortals to plant and harvest and grind the wheat. She had instructed them about plants whose leaves and roots cured illness. There was no winter in those days, only the cycles of growth and decay.

Persephone and Her Mother Demeter especially loved the flowers. They gathered the blossoms of narcissus and hyacinth, myrtle and poppies, and wove garlands for their hair. When They danced together on the hillsides, tiny green shoots would spring up in Their footprints.

One day Persephone asked Her Mother about the spirits of the dead. "Who receives them," She asked, "when they enter the netherworld?" Demeter sighed and explained that She Herself was responsible for the underworld, that She had taught the humans to store seed under the earth so that contact with the spirits of the underworld would fertilize the seed. But She added that Her most important task was to feed the living.

Persephone decided to make the long journey into the netherworld. "I will go to the dead," She said. "They need us."

Demeter reminded Her Daughter of the warmth and light and flowers They enjoyed. She begged Her not to enter the dark and gloomy underworld. But Persephone had decided to go. Demeter understood but She knew She would grieve for Her Daughter until She returned. As Persephone started down into the deep chasm in the earth, She carried three poppies and three sheaves of wheat. Demeter gave her a torch to light the way. Persephone walked for many hours into the darkness until She came to a great wide space where the spirits of the dead were moaning in despair.

Persephone moved among the spirits and stepped up onto a large flat rock. She brought forth a great bowl of pomegranate seeds, the food of the dead. She welcomed the spirits to their new world, embracing each one and painting each forehead with the red juice of the pomegranate seeds. She stayed for many months.

Demeter grieved as She knew She would. As the weeks and months passed She withdrew Her energy from the plants and the crops. No new growth appeared. In Her loneliness Demeter could only sit on the hillside and wait.

Finally one morning Demeter felt the warm breeze whisper "Persephone returns!" Demeter's energy burst forth and everywhere new life began to appear as She ran down the hill crying "Persephone returns!" When Persephone came forth from the underworld, She ran to Demeter and They hugged and cried and danced. The humans felt everywhere the new life of spring. Each year when Persephone descends to the underworld there is the bleak winter of Demeter's grief. Each year when Persephone returns there is the spring of joyful new life as Mother and Daughter are reunited.[4]

Notice that in this version of the myth Persephone decides for herself that she must leave her mother and embark upon her own spiritual journey. Demeter fears for her, grieves at her absence, but knows that the journey is necessary. Ultimately Persephone returns to her mother, transformed into an adult by her journey, and they rejoice in a new kind of relationship. The structure of the myth as told above is based upon Charlene Spretnak's careful research into the very earliest versions of the story.[5]

In the later, patriarchal version of the myth as it has come down to us, Persephone is captured and carried off by force. She does not make her own decision and Demeter is more angry than grieving. The daughter is never allowed to grow into her true self and her relationship with her mother is strained and arbitrary.

Think again of your own mother. Make a list of the positive effects she had on your life. Make a list of the negative effects. How do you feel about the life she lived? Does your knowledge of your grandmother help you to understand your mother? What would you wish now for your relationship with your mother? Say to yourself "The Goddess affirms the relationship between mothers and daughters."

Another aspect of our problem as adult women and as mothers and daughters is that in our society only young women are desirable or valued at all. Older women try to look young because they know they are not wanted if they are old. This attitude was not part of the ancient Goddess religions. These myths celebrated not only the maiden and the mother but also the crone or wise old woman who had much to teach.

According to Barbara Walker the Crone was the aspect of the Goddess most completely obliterated by patriarchal religion because men found it the most intimidating and powerful.6 She represented death. Death in the old religions was a natural part of life. As Demeter explains in the myth, seed was stored beneath the surface of the earth so that contact with the spirits of the underworld would fertilize the seed. Patriarchal religions tend to deny death and so to fear and deny the power of the Crone who can destroy.

The waxing, full and waning moon, so closely related to woman's menstrual cycle, was used also to symbolize the life stages of woman.

Sit comfortably now in front of your lighted candle and breathe deeply. In the Old Religion the Moon Goddess has three aspects: as She waxes, She is the Maiden; as She is full, She is the Mother; as She wanes, She is the Crone.

Visualize now the waxing crescent moon which curves to the right. See the Young Girl dancing freely in the night. She belongs to no one but herself. She holds within herself all potential, all creative possibility. She is your plans, your dreams, your hopes, your undiscovered self waiting to be made manifest.

Visualize the full moon, round and gleaming. See the fullness of the Mother. She gives life and brings forth all manner of creative gifts. She is your sexual self fulfilled. She is your pleasure, your power to love and to create and nurture life.

Visualize the waning crescent moon which curves to the left. See the Crone, the old woman of wisdom and of death. She brings knowledge of the mystery that death is part of the great cycle of life. She is your power to end, to let go of what is no longer healthy. She is your strength for meeting the transformations of life and of death. The Goddess, She Who is the potential of the Maiden and the fullness of the Mother and the power of the Crone, affirms women of all ages.

Say aloud: The Goddess affirms women of all ages.

SIX

Why Did It Happen?
The Shift From Goddess To God

BEFORE YOU BEGIN this chapter, get yourself a fist-sized lump of clay and place it beside your special candle. When you are ready, light your candle, breathe deeply and read the following poem by Marge Piercy:

The bonsai tree
in the attractive pot
could have grown eighty feet tall
on the side of a mountain
till split by lightning.
But a gardener
carefully pruned it.
It is nine inches high
Every day as he
whittles back the branches
the gardener croons,
It is your nature
to be small and cozy,
domestic and weak;

how lucky, little tree,
to have a pot to grow in.
With living creatures
one must begin very early
to dwarf their growth:
the bound feet,
the crippled brain,
the hair in curlers,
the hands you
love to touch.[1]

Now take the clay and mold into it something about who you are. What are your strengths and weaknesses as a person? What are some of your values? Allow yourself about fifteen minutes to work with the clay, longer if you wish. When you have finished, write down in a sentence or two exactly what you have tried to express with the clay.

We return now to the issue of power, to ask how women lost power in the course of human history and how women lose or give away power in their personal lives today.

Ancient mythologies from many cultures reflect a shift in divine power from the female to the male. For many thousands of years human beings rested comfortably in the lap of the great Mother Goddess. There were male sons and consorts, but the Mother was all-embracing. Gradually the male deities became stronger and took on more and more power. The Goddesses became less important or were transformed into petulant or evil forces. In some myths there were great battles between the male gods and the older Goddesses; in other myths the Goddesses bestowed their power on male consorts who then became the chief deities. If we accept the theory that myths reflect the power structures of societies, it follows that women had significant power in the early history of humanity but had that power wrested away in a long struggle.

In Babylonia the Goddess was known as Tiamat. Her story is told in the epic poem Enuma Elish. Tiamat's grandson, Marduk, called by the poet "the wisest of the gods" engages Tiamat in one to one combat. Marduk uses all manner of trickery and evil to defeat her. He enmeshes her in a net and causes "an evil wind" to blow in her face. When Tiamat opens her mouth to devour him he drives the wind into her belly. With her belly distended and her mouth open Tiamat is then torn apart by the arrow Marduk shoots into her interior. After she is subdued he casts down her body and with his club splits her skull. The poet happily concludes "When his fathers saw this, they were glad and rejoiced...The lord rested, examining her dead body."[2]

Athena, whose roots were in Minoan Crete, was captured but then allowed herself to be transformed into a Goddess acceptable to a patriarchal society.

The Myth of Athena

The Goddess Athena had her origins in Minoan Crete where the Great Goddess is shown with life-renewing serpents curled about her arms and a wise owl perched upon her head. There Athena presided over the emergence of a high civilization. Athena's people learned to keep written records, to paint elegant frescoes for their carefully designed and storied buildings, and to live in peace with their neighbors for a thousand years. The Minoans had no fortifications. Athena protected them with her invincible aura. Their shipping trade prospered and all the arts flourished in an atmosphere of peace and plenty. The making of gold vessels and jewelry, weaving and pottery, all were taught and nurtured by the lovely and powerful Goddess.

In time, however, even the power of Athena could not protect this beautiful civilization. Fierce northern invaders swept over the island. Athena was carried off to Attica where she was made to don a helmet, and to hold forth a shield and a sword.[3]

Still Athena retained much power, and one of the most beautiful temples of all time was built in Her honor, the Parthenon. Nor was the Goddess religion limited to ancient Europe and the Near East. Images of the Goddess appear in every culture around the world. In the Greek world she was sometimes known as Artemis. She appears in Yugoslavia, Peru and in Tibet where she was known as Tara. In China she was Kuan Yin, Goddess of Mercy. In Japan she was the Sun Goddess, Amaterasu. She appears among the Celts, the Aztecs who called her Tlazolteotl, and in the Congo.

Then at the close of the Bronze Age, over a period of one to three thousand years, the patriarchal deities battled the Great Goddess and all She represented. Early representations of the Goddess often show Her with a son or consort, always smaller and often protected by Her. Later, the male god is depicted as larger than the female.

In the early stages of patriarchy while men were still in awe of the Goddess, male and female deities often reigned together. But as time went by the shrines of the Goddess were mutilated. Her priestesses dispersed and Her power was obliterated. The male deities became more and more powerful, even taking over the creative functions of the female, so that we encounter distortions of mythic symbols, to say nothing of distortions of reality, such as the births of Eve from Adam's rib and Athena from Zeus's head.

By 500 C.E. when patriarchal Christianity held sway, the last of the Goddess temples had been destroyed or converted to Christian holy places. In the myths of transition some Goddesses had their power taken from them by force and were brutally dismembered, like Tiamat. Other Goddesses, like Athena, were tricked into giving their power away, conferring it upon kings or becoming consorts of the new male deities, retaining some limited power but gradually becoming personifications of evil or objects of hatred. Women entered a long dark age of powerlessness. From being human representatives of divine creativity and procreativity, women became human representatives of evil, lust and sin.

The big question of course is why? Why did men need to gain control and why did women allow it to happen? Three major theories have been put forth.

I. Rebellion against a Matriarchy

In the late nineteenth century Jacob Bachofen and others suggested that human society had evolved through two stages before it became patriarchal.[4] The first stage was a time of sexual promiscuity and disorder. When that stage became intolerable, the mothers established a matriarchal rule in order to protect and provide for the children. Men were treated as inferior, and their only access to power was through their sisters. When this system became intolerable, the men overthrew the matriarchy and established male rule. Patriarchy was considered by Bachofen to be a higher form of society. It did not occur to him that it, too, might become intolerable. Anthropologists of the late nineteenth century and early twentieth century quickly criticized Bachofen's ideas about matriarchy as unscientific and not supported by the archeological evidence. Later in the twentieth century the archeological evidence for female power in ancient societies became overwhelming. The evidence, however, does not seem to support the notion of a matriarchal society. Riane

Eisler in her book, *The Chalice and the Blade, Our History, Our Future*[5] has suggested that ancient societies had a system of shared power between women and men, that they were neither patriarchal nor matriarchal, but organized on a model of partnership rather than a model of domination.

II. Progress into an "Adult" Society

Another theory to explain the shift in power is based on Jungian psychology and makes an analogy between individual development and societal development. An individual is completely nurtured and cared for by her or his mother early in life. Later, in order to grow, she or he must grow out of infant bliss and go into the father's world. The assumption, of course, is that the adult world is a male one. Similarly the human species first revered only female power; later it had to separate itself from female deities and turn to male gods. Again, the shift from female to male identification is seen as an evolution to a higher form of religion and society, with little awareness that a shift to patriarchy may be regressive or that the future may demand further change. For a detailed and excellent presentation of this theory see Erich Neumann's *The Great Mother*.[6] Criticisms of Jungian theory can be found in Spretnak's introduction to *Lost Goddesses of Early Greece*[7] and in Goldenberg's *Changing of the Gods*.[8]

III. Invasion and Cultural Domination

Merlin Stone offers a third theory in *When God Was A Woman*.[9] She traces the known and hypothesized migrations of early people and suggests that waves of Indo-Europeans surged southward and conquered and merged with the inhabitants of the Ancient Near East and the

Mediterranean region. These Indo-Europeans were nomadic herders, unlike the settled agricultural peoples they conquered. Their chief gods were male and their society was patriarchal, whereas the agricultural peoples worshipped a Goddess and had a matrifocal or possibly a matriarchal society. When the Indo-Europeans merged with the locals the myths of the two cultures coexisted, but the conquering male gods eventually gained prominence.

We are left with many questions, but the important fact for women is that we lost our power and that we need to reclaim it in creative ways in the modern world. Patriarchy, however it came into being, has now become intolerable and is in a state of decline. Like the ancient Goddesses who had their power taken from them in fierce battles or who "voluntarily" bestowed it on males, we in our personal lives are sometimes forcibly deprived of power and sometimes collaborate in giving it away. We need to be aware of what we do with the personal power that is rightfully ours.

Perhaps the most obvious way in which modern women have power forcibly taken from them is through the violence of men toward women. Thousands of women are terrorized in their own homes by men who profess to love them. They suffer broken bones, extensive bruises and concussions. Many are murdered when they try to escape. Only in very recent years have such women had safe shelters to which they can go with their children. The irony even then is that the abused and beaten wife must leave her home while the abusing husband or lover is free to continue his lifestyle and live in the family home. Even women who are not abused are afraid that if they assert themselves they might be in danger. Many women clients I have seen in therapy have admitted, when pressed, the reason they are afraid: "Well, after all, he's bigger than I am."

Rape is another form of violence against women. It most often goes unpunished because few women who have already been humiliated by the rape itself will risk the heavy bias against them in the justice system. A woman who charges a man with rape is subjected to questioning which implies that she is immoral and provoked the rape, or really wanted to have sex with the offender even if she said no. In the film *Thelma and Louise* one woman shoots and kills the rapist-attacker of her friend. Knowing the bias of the justice system, the two women decide to try to escape to Mexico. In a series of tragic but hilarious escapades the women learn to wield guns and to put a variety of obnoxious men in their places. But the chilling message of the film is that there is no escape. Caught between an army of police (representing a justice system stacked against them) and the rim of the Grand Canyon, Thelma and Louise gun the car and drive over the edge. The image recurs as bumper stickers proclaim: Thelma and Louise Live. As an image of the plight of women who fight back when raped, they do indeed live.

Pornography too reinforces the degradation and power-lessness of women. It does not portray love and erotic pleasure but rather the contempt and domination of one sex over the other.

In patriarchal societies around the world women have been forcibly kept powerless—by witch hunts in Europe and America, foot-binding in China, widow burning in India, gynecological surgery in America, genital mutilation in Africa. Our bodies are still not our own when governments are allowed to decide for us whether and under what circumstances we will bear children. Women have been denied citizenship and suffrage right down to modern times. In the United States women are still not guaranteed equal rights under the law and the law is backed up by force.

Harder to discern are the ways we women have of giving our power away. Take humor, jokes, for example. Have you ever noticed how many jokes are considered funny because they ridicule or demean women? I remember a young man, a psychology intern, who came to work one day wearing a tie with a tiny pig embroidered on it. Under the pig were the neatly stitched words "I'm an M.C.P." (Male Chauvinist Pig) Several women psychologists and social workers were gathered around him, laughing at the tie. I didn't think it was funny. I asked him if he would wear a tie that said "I'm a racist." I said that his tie was just that offensive to me as a woman. The laughter stopped. Nobody said anything more about the tie and the young man never wore it to work again. I didn't like having to stop the laughter and comraderie. I knew there had been a long time in my life when I would not have recognized the tie as offensive. I might have laughed too, even if I had felt strangely uneasy doing so. But, once aware of the insult, not to object to the tie would have been to perpetuate the insult, to condone sexism as cute or funny, *to give away my power as a woman.* My power to speak my truth.

Many of us who chose to combine marriage with a career back in the fifties assumed that we had to continue doing all the cooking, laundry and other housework in addition to our outside careers. We never thought to negotiate with our husbands to share those burdens. After all, he was tired after a day at work. As if we weren't! But when our consciousness began to be raised and we spoke up, many husbands agreed to change the old patterns. Once we were aware of the extra burdens as unfair, not asserting ourselves would have meant giving away our power as women.

Many women in the business world used to find that they were expected to do certain tasks that never appeared in their job descriptions—everything from making coffee to having sex with the boss. Not making coffee became the symbolic act of liberation for many female administrative assistants. I had a little button I used to wear that said

"Women: Make policy, not coffee." I wore it one day to a meeting of the child study team in a junior high school. The principal was there and he leaned across his desk to read the button. Right at that moment his female secretary opened the door and carried in a tray of coffee and cups. The principal turned red, grabbed the tray and served the coffee himself. Without the button, or someone to speak up, nobody might have noticed that the secretary was giving away her power as a woman.

We may no longer make the coffee but sexual harassment continues unabated. Many women were deeply moved by Anita Hill's courage in coming forward to tell her story during the Clarence Thomas confirmation hearings, and deeply angered by the way she was treated as she faced an all-male line-up of Senators. She refused to give away her power by keeping silent and the image of a beautiful, highly educated black woman sitting alone opposite those white male Senators hour after hour is permanently engraved in our consciousness as women. More and more women now are claiming their own power and finding the strength to speak out against the sexual harassment they have experienced.

A less obvious way that we may give away our power is in accepting the way men define an issue or a question. Jean Baker Miller points out that women who wish to pursue a career are often asked "How do you propose to answer the need for child care?" She suggests that we need to re-phrase the question and ask "If we as a human community want children, how does the total society propose to provide for them? How can it provide for them in such a way that women do not have to suffer or forfeit other forms of participation and power? How does society propose to organize so that men can benefit from equal participation in child care?"[10]

In early 1993 the confirmation hearings for Zoe Baird, President Clinton's first nominee for Attorney General, made it abundantly clear that this society does not provide for children "in such a way that women do not have to suffer or forfeit other forms of participation and power." Ms. Baird was forced to withdraw from the nomination after it was revealed that she had hired an illegal immigrant to provide child care. There is not adequate child care in this country, even for an affluent woman like Ms. Baird! Notably, Baird's husband, a law professor at an Ivy League institution, was not subjected to the same ethical scrutiny as the assumption continues to be that all child care arrangements are the responsibility of the mother, who, by choosing to work, is abandoning her primary role.

Resorting to an illegal arrangement certainly is not an acceptable solution. Zoe Baird had accepted the patriarchal way of asking the question about child care, the way that assumed that child care was entirely her problem. Instead of organizing other professional women to demand that adequate legal child care be made available, she resorted to hiring someone illegally. Perhaps she is not an organizer. Perhaps that is not how she wished to use her energies. Perhaps she never thought to redefine the question.

And no one has ever asked a male Cabinet nominee what he does about child care.

Think now about your own life. At what points have you experienced power being taken away from you? At what points have you given your power away? Think of the qualities of self you molded into your clay. In the future, what can you do to claim your rightful power as a woman? Jot down your ideas. Now breathe deeply and read aloud the following passage:

Hear the words of the Star Goddess, the dust of whose feet are the hosts of heaven, whose body encircles the universe: I who am the beauty of the green Earth and the white moon among the stars and the mysteries of the waters, I call upon your soul to arise and come unto Me. For I am the soul of nature that gives life to the universe. From Me all things proceed and unto Me they must return. Let My worship be in the heart that rejoices, for behold—all acts of love and pleasure are My rituals. Let there be beauty and strength, power and compassion, honor and humility, mirth and reverence within you. And you who seek to know Me, know that your seeking and yearning will avail you not, unless you know the Mystery: for if that which you seek you find not within yourself, you will never find it without. For behold, I have been with you from the beginning, and I am that which is attained at the end of desire.[11]

SEVEN

Reclaiming
the Female Presence in Judaism

TO BEGIN THIS CHAPTER you will need to have a honey cake or other sweet pastry, some fresh fruit or other special treat to place beside your candle. Find a large piece of drawing paper and a box of crayons. Light your special candle and take a few deep breaths. As you read the next three paragraphs, allow yourself to be in touch with your feelings, letting them absorb you.

It is the winners who write history and proclaim new myths that support that history. We have seen that as the great Goddesses were defeated and replaced by male gods in the ancient world, women lost significant political and social power. All the history and mythology that has been handed down to us has been rewritten from the male point of view. Female images of the Divine and the voices of women in history have been carefully edited out of the human story or minimized. They are described as primitive, evil, or decadent. The Bible clearly follows this pattern. As Judaism developed its clear and powerful concept of ethical monotheism, all positive references to the earlier worship of a Goddess were edited out of the scripture.

Although traditional Judaism denies that God has physical traits and insists that God could be neither male nor female, language has defied all these theological statements. The two biblical names for God, Yahweh and Elohim, are masculine and in Hebrew require masculine pronouns, verbs and adjectives. Every statement about God conveys the idea that he is masculine. No subsequent theological teaching can eradicate this mental image acquired in early childhood. For the most part, no attempt was made to counteract it, and all the prophets, psalmists, and scribes use masculine phrases such as "Man of War," "Hero," "Lord of Hosts," "King," "Our Father," to refer to God. The god of Judaism is a great father symbol, and it is that father symbol that we have accepted (or rejected) as the one and only God. Human beings, however, have an equally great need for a female symbol, the Divine woman who appears in many forms all over the world. Judaism, gradually developed and strictly monotheistic, focuses on a god described by scriptures in masculine terms, thus reflecting the patriarchal society that produced it. The popular religion of the people, referred to and preached against in the scriptures, reflects the practice of earlier times, when the Divine female reigned beside Yahweh and when women were prophets and judges.

As contemporary women we may cherish the ethical monotheism proclaimed by the prophets, but we need to question the exclusively male symbolism in which it is couched. We need to ask whether or not something of value was lost when female references to the Divine were excluded and women came to be denied positions of leadership in our society as well as in our myths.

Now take the crayons and express on paper your feelings about those three paragraphs. Use any creative way that appeals to you. Allow yourself plenty of time, and use the colors to show any conflicting or ambiguous feelings you may have. Then jot down in words what you tried to express in your drawing. What has been your experience of the biblical god? What kind of understanding of the Divine do you have? Is it changing? Why?

Most of us grew up within a branch of Judaism or Christianity, and all of us in Western society were raised in a culture heavily influenced and undergirded by the assumptions of Judaism and Christianity. Many of us have rejected the biblical traditions and turned to other religions or to secular sources for inspiration; others have rejected only certain aspects of the biblical tradition and would like to be identified with its message of love and justice.

Let us now look at the biblical tradition within the context of the many thousands of years of human religious history that preceded it and the rich religious traditions of the cultures that surrounded it. We have been taught to take a very bigoted and condescending view of "pagan" traditions. The perspective I suggest here is that Judaism was greatly enriched by its interactions with Canaanite religion for many centuries and may have lost something of value in its drive to edit "foreign" elements out of the scriptures.

The Bible was written and rewritten during the very centuries when Goddesses were in combat with male deities throughout the Ancient Near East and women were losing their earlier power. From this perspective much of the Bible, especially the scriptures of Judaism can be read as a polemic against the old Goddess religions and a powerful voice supporting the new patriarchal deities. Indeed, it went much further than other religious myths of its time. Ultimately it took the radical position that Yahweh was not only the most powerful deity but the only one. Other male deities of the time took only the top position in a pantheon and relegated the old Goddesses to lesser positions. The Bible took the most radically patriarchal position possible.

Liberal theology has long insisted that the scriptures have to be understood within the context of the historical era in which they were written. Until recently, however, most biblical scholarship ignored the long shift in Divine power, from female to male, that was taking place in the Ancient Near East when the Bible was being written. Raphael Patai has explored that historical fact as a central issue in understanding the Bible; this chapter draws heavily on his work.[1] It is an issue of particular importance to women as we try to relate the Bible to our own experience.

If the gods have changed in the past they can change again. Is it possible to claim the biblical heritage for women? What kind of changes are necessary in our understanding of the Divine? Naomi Goldenberg takes the position that God must be understood today in psychological terms, as internal, a power of selfhood within us.[2] For women, then, the god within must be female. Other women see the Divine as residing in all of nature, including ourselves. Now is the time for you to explore your own personal understandings of the Divine.

Look again at the feelings you expressed in response to the reading about female references being edited out of the Bible. It is important to understand that our voices as women, our contributions to today's society are still being ignored, neglected or actively edited out. Good ideas expressed by women are often stolen or co-opted so that a man takes the credit. Many women have told me of committee or task force meetings where a woman presents an idea or makes a suggestion. She is ignored, but a few minutes later a man repeats the idea or suggestion as his own and everyone accepts and praises it. He gets the credit. If she objects she is seen as "a prima dona." Isn't the use of a good idea more important than who gets the credit? Perhaps. But such stealing perpetuates the stereotype of woman as inferior, man as having the most important ideas.

As women we are "edited out" every day in conversations with men. Men interrupt more, monopolize more, and talk louder to drown out an opponent. They are frequently admired for this aggressive "leadership." I have noticed that if a woman behaves in a similar fashion, say by interrupting a man repeatedly, she is not only not admired but may be severely criticized. Or expected to feel guilty when the man says in consternation "Let me finish!" Much has been written about the importance of listening. It is important, but women have done far too much listening. We need to know the importance of speaking up. We need to learn how to make ourselves heard.

As women we have a long history of contributions in every area of human culture. We didn't really know that in the early days of women's studies. We believed what we had been taught—that women were an insignificant set of footnotes to the major contributions of men. A seminar or two, not required of course, would cover what women had done. But the more we looked, the more we found that women had always been there and even against incredible odds had produced literature and art and science of impressive quality and quantity. The problem was that these works were not mentioned in our educational system.

Most of us have taken high school and college courses where women were not mentioned at all. I remember one in particular because I took it at a time when I was becoming aware of the glaring absence of women. The course was about the work of theologian Ernst Troelstch. He wrote volumes and we read volumes and nowhere did he ever once mention women. So I said that one day in class. A male student said dryly "No, you're wrong. On page 456 of volume two he has a footnote where he mentions women." It is interesting too that full semester courses were offered on each important male theologian while all the female theologians, if taught at all, were lumped together in one course, not required.

The "editing out" process sometimes happens in the most blatant open manner. In 1976, the bicentennial of the Declaration of Independence, I went to hear a distinguished professor of history speak at a church service. He had a most interesting thesis—that the Revolution was not a one-time event, but an ongoing process. As an example he used the right to vote, pointing out that at first only landowners could vote. Then he spoke eloquently about how that right had been extended to non-landowners, then to blacks and finally to Native Americans. Then he concluded his talk and asked for questions. I thought that surely someone would ask about the incredible omission of women's suffrage. No one did. So I very reluctantly did. He smiled benignly and said "Oh, well I thought the ladies could speak for themselves." He nodded quickly to the organist who began the closing hymn. Indeed, we do need to speak for ourselves. At the coffee hour I found myself surrounded by women who said they too had noticed the omission in his talk but were afraid to say anything. Each woman thought she was the only one who noticed. If I hadn't spoken they would never have known they shared that experience. In the words of an old song "silence like a cancer grows."

Perhaps the most subtle and insidious "editing out" happens in our use of language. Theodora Wells, in an exercise on awareness wrote: "Consider changing the title of a university course to 'Humanistic Images of Woman,' using the term woman as a general term meaning both women and men! Feel that, sense its meaning to you as a woman...Think of it being that way, every day of your life. Feel the ever-presence of woman and feel the nonpresence of man. Absorb what it tells you about the importance and value of being woman, of being man."[3] Such exercises in reversal can sometimes shock us into awareness. When this nations's founding fathers said all men were created equal, they meant white men who owned land. If they had meant to include the rest of us we would all have been able to vote right from the beginning. The pervasive use of the male pronoun as generic molds our thinking from childhood on so that we take for granted the nonpresence of woman. We don't even notice. *We are not told the whole story.*

We need very much to reclaim the lost female heritage that was edited out of the biblical tradition. Whether or not we wish to remain within that tradition we need once again to know the whole story.

Let's journey again into the past, back to the time when the Hebrew people first settled in the land of Canaan. From about 1200 B.C.E. down to the Babylonian exile in 586 B.C.E. the children of Israel worshipped the Goddess Asherah who was the chief Goddess of the Canaanite pantheon. We need to understand that gods and Goddesses are rarely invented; usually they are taken over by one group from another. Even Yahweh had pre-Hebrew antecedents, and the worship of various Canaanite deities became an integral part of the religion of the Hebrews for many centuries. Raphael Patai writes, "There can be no doubt that the Goddess to whom the Hebrews clung with such tenacity down to the days of Josiah, and to whom they returned with such remorse following the destruction of the Jerusalem Temple was, whatever the prophets had to say about her, no foreign seductress but a

Hebrew Goddess, the best divine mother the people had to that time."[4]

At Ras Shamra, near the northeastern corner of the Mediterranean, tablets were discovered written in a language similar to biblical Hebrew and dating to the fourteenth century B.C.E. These tablets provide rich mythical material about the early Canaanite religion. Asherah was the chief Goddess and the wife of El, the chief god. She was also referred to simply as Elath or Goddess. She was the progenitress of the gods, and all the other deities were Her children. The most popular of Her children were her son, Hadd, who was also called Baal or Lord, and Her daughter, Anath. Asherah was associated with a number of cities, so there were Asherahs of many localities, just as there is a Virgin of Fatima, a Virgin of Guadelupe, and so on. When biblical references say the Israelites served "the Asherahs" it means they worshipped several of these local manifestations of the Great Goddess. As the Israelites and Canaanites intermarried, the Bible reports that "the Children of Israel...served the Baals and the Asherahs."

Biblical references to Asherah indicate that large, wooden images of the Goddess were carved and implanted in the ground. Later a statue of Asherah was set up in the Jerusalem temple. The wooden images of the Goddess have not survived, but small clay images used in homes were found in every excavation in the Holy Land. These had a flared base so they could be placed upright. They are thought to be similar to the large wooden images used in public places.

Often Asherah is shown holding flowers or standing on a lion. She is sometimes referred to as Queen of the Wild Beasts. In many parts of the ancient world she was called the Queen of Heaven. In an unusual passage in the book of the prophet Jeremiah, the ritual used for worship of the Queen of Heaven is outlined. God speaks to Jeremiah, saying "Do you not see what they do in the cities of Judah and in the streets of Jerusalem? The children gather wood and the fathers kindle the fire, and the women knead the dough to make cakes to the Queen of Heaven, and they pour out libations to other gods, in order to anger me!"[5]

Jeremiah warns the people that if they do not stop this worship and turn only to Yahweh, a great catastrophe will occur. The catastrophe does occur and they are driven into exile in Egypt. Jeremiah reminds them of his warning, saying that their exile is punishment for their worship of the Queen of Heaven. But the people interpret the catastrophe in the opposite way. Their answer to Jeremiah is "As for the word that you have spoken to us in the name of Yahweh—we shall not listen to you. But we shall without fail do everything as we said: we shall burn incense to the Queen of Heaven, and shall pour her libations as we used to do, we, our fathers, our kings and our princes, in the cities of Judah and in the streets of Jerusalem. For then we had plenty of food, and we all were well and saw no evil. But since we ceased burning incense to the Queen of Heaven and to pour her libations, we have wanted everything and have been consumed by sword and famine."[6]

Later, when strict monotheism triumphed, the Divine female remained only in spirit as the Shekhina, or "presence of God." God's actual presence with the Children of Israel was imagined to be somewhat distinct from God himself and was spoken of in female terms as the Shekhina. This female presence became a primary focus again many centuries later in medieval Jewish mysticism.

In *Changing of the Gods* [7] Naomi Goldenberg speculates about the future of religion today. She imagines that as feminism advances, women will become priests, ministers and rabbis. If that happens, she wonders, wouldn't God begin to look like "His" female representatives? This thought brings her to the conclusion that God will have to change, that as women claim their rightful places in government, in the arts and professions and in religion, the world will be so different that God "won't fit in anymore." Feeling no sense of loss about God's cultural demise, Goldenberg instead expresses her exhilaration at being part of a movement "that would challenge religions that had been in force for millennia." Then she poses the logical next question: "Who or what will replace Him?"

Is Goldenberg right in saying that God will have to change? What might the new deity be like? What kind of changes do you think must occur today in order for women to be truly included in religion and in society? Take some time to ponder these questions as you enjoy your special candle and your honey cake.

EIGHT

Discovering
the Voices of Women in Judaism

LIGHT YOUR CANDLE and think for a moment of your own experience with Bible stories. Who are the women you remember from those stories? How much do their stories tell you about their thoughts and feelings as women? Monique Wittig has suggested that if our history as women has been lost, if we cannot remember it no matter how hard we try, that we should "invent."[1]

Women today who identify strongly with the great themes of love and justice in the biblical tradition are using their own experience as women to invent, that is, to rewrite some of the stories in the Bible as they might have been told by the women involved. Elinor Artman has retold the story of Hosea and his wife Gomar from Gomar's point of view:

Between Two Gods

For millennia Hosea has had his say about his marriage, using it as an allegory for the relationship between YHWH and

Israel. Unlike angry Amos, who prophesied doom with the voice of an irate and vengeful God, Hosea and his God spoke with a suffering and sorrowing voice, still irate and vengeful to be sure, but tempered with steadfast loving kindness. But what of the Canaanite Gods with whom YHWH struggles in the hearts of the people—Lady Asherah and her beloved son Baal? Perhaps it is time for Gomar, Hosea's wife, to respond.

Gomar speaks:

Oh, gentle and loving husband.
Oh, bitter and wrathful husband.
Oh, Hosea, prophet of YHWH.
    You have tried to save your people from the ire of
    your God.
    I have tried to help my people rejoice in thanksgiving
    for our God.
You came as stranger to our land.
You brought your God with you.
But we had our God already—Lady Asherah.
Somehow we could not live side by side.
Honoring each other.
Honoring each other's God.

Your God became jealous and possessive.
Was it from fear?
Was it from fear of the greater power of our Asherah?
Why could they not share the power?
Was it from fear?
You knew who I was when you came.
Yet you came and wooed me.

I was one of the chosen ones.
A temple priestess of Asherah.
    An upright and religious woman, entrusted
to enact the most
ancient fertility rites with petitioners and pilgrims.

Without those rites the earth would not be
    renewed once more,
Would not be returned to fertility once again.
Drought and famine would rule us.
Hunger and fear would capture us.
Sorrow and death would reign.

And then you came.
And you wooed me.
And I fell from grace.
You were handsome and a stranger.
I was, they say, beautiful and honored among women.

I was happy and content in my service to Asherah and to
    my people.
You came and you wooed me.
You pleaded with me.
You promised me your God, your God of justice and
    loving kindness.
You promised me treasures, silver and gold, oils
    and wines,
More than Asherah had ever given me.
You said your God had sent you.
You said you would rescue me from Asherah.
You promised me yourself as well.

And so I loved you.
And so I deserted Asherah.
And so I fell from grace.
For a while we were happy.
Safe in our own dream world.
Hiding from our Gods.
Who can hide from a God?
Not even we.

The words of Amos, the angry one, reached you.
And the tales of his prophecies.

And tales of how the people jeered and defiled him.
Amos's messages had fallen on deaf ears.
For they were spoken in good times,
In times of peace and prosperity.
Who could hear the voice of doom then?
Who could heed warnings when blessings abound?
But your God whispered to you, Hosea.
The day of the fall was closer.
You could see the signs.
Your God whispered to you, Hosea:
"I am a God of justice and vengeance, a God of Amos.
But I am a God of kindness also, a God of Hosea.
Go tell my people, Hosea.
Recall them to the Covenant.
A new voice is needed.
You, Hosea, must now speak for me."

Alas for us Hosea.
Your God whispered and you listened.
The new voice was to be yours.
So you left me for a new bride.
You left me for Israel.
And I was alone and bereft.
You became a stranger to me once again.

Even our children you named strange names.
Jazreel, God sows, you called our first born to remind
    us of the bloody doom of Jezabel and of the priests
    of Baal.
Loruhamah, not loved, you called our daughter
    to remind us that YHWH was unloving and unforgiving.
Loammi, not mine, you called our youngest
    to remind us that we were deserted and disowned.
Ah, my poor innocent beloved babes.
Where was your father's loving kindness then?
And our story, yours and mine, Hosea, you turned into

a tale of YHWH and Israel.

With you as YHWH (of course), the suffering and
sorrowing master.

And I as Israel, the errant wife and servant.

Alas, alas.

Oh, Asherah, I forsook you.

For what? For what?

Where is this justice and love of YHWH?

I feel only sorrow and loneliness.

Forgive me, forgive me, oh Asherah.

And lo, Asherah whispered in my ear:

"Come back, O daughter,

I am a forgiving Goddess.

I have missed you.

You were among my favored ones.

Come back, my daughter.

You served me well."

So I returned to Asherah.

To my service in Asherah's temple and festivals.

Oils and wines, gold and silver, grains and corn
were mine once again.

And an honored place with my Lady and my people.

I returned to Asherah, my renewer.

And she received me with comfort and rejoicing.

But I have lost you for all time, Hosea. Or is it
that you have lost me?

We are parted.

Perhaps in another world...

Are our Gods so different?

Must it be one or the other?

Can we not dwell together in harmony?

Is Asherah so different from the Gods of your
ancestors, Hosea?

Those people who roamed the land even before the

time of Abraham.

Those who sensed manna in sacred outcrops of the
desert and in the trees of the oases.

Those who ventured stone pillars and burning bushes
and cajoled the spirits of the sandstorms and
of the night.

Those who wooed the life-giving rain and the renewal
of the earth.

Were they so different? Elshaddai and Asherah?

The Divinity of the Mountains and the God of the Air
and Rain.

Oh, Hosea, you do what you must do.

I do what I must do.

We must each serve our Gods in our way, and try to
rejoice in that.

I will not be bitter.

Bitter fruits are unbecoming to a priestess
of Asherah.

Be thou likewise not bitter.

Forgive me as I forgive you.

Even as our Gods, the great YHWH and the great
Asherah forgive us.

May they live side by side.

Although I know in my heart that may never be,
I still pray for it.

For Gods are ever jealous and eternally struggle
for dominance.

Even as men and women do.

But the day of harmony may come yet. I still pray
for it.

I continue to hope, as I know you do.

Life would indeed be harsh, if love and kindness and
hope were gone.

And you, even in your despair and love may remember
the earth and sing as YHWH did once:
"I will be as the dew to Israel;
he shall blossom as the lily
he shall strike root as the poplar;
his shoots shall spread out;
his beauty shall be like the olive, and
his fragrance like Lebanon.
They shall return and dwell beneath my shadow,
They shall flourish as a garden;
They shall blossom as the vine,
Their fragrance shall be like the wine of Lebanon.
I am like an evergreen cypress.
From me comes your fruit."

And I, even in my love and despair may remember the
heavens and sing as Asherah once did:
"Now do thou banish warfare from the earth,
And love do thou implant within the land!
Now do thou weave no longer on the earth
Tissues of hate, but rather threads of peace:
I bid thee, twine no longer in the land
a mesh of guile, but rather skeins of love!
Lo, I, installed as godhead of the north,
Will fashion now upon that hill of mine
A lightning such as heaven never heard,
Greater than all mankind yet understand."

And some day your world-transcending God will be reconciled with my world-renewing God, peace shall reign, and we shall be together again in the land.[2]

Now it is your turn. Bring your own imagination, experience and creativity to a new form of Bible study. Women did not write the books of the Bible, and the female point of view is glaringly absent. But there are women in the Bible, some obviously very strong and wise. Can we use our imaginations to put them back in the story? On the basis of our own experience can we imagine what they might have felt, thought, or said? And as we do that, will we interpret the Bible differently? Will our understanding of the divine, of God, change?

Here is the story of Abraham, Sarah and Isaac:

"After these things God tested Abraham, and said to him, `Abraham!' And he said, `Here am I.' He said, `Take your son, your only son Isaac, whom you love, and go to the land of Moriah, and offer him there as a burnt offering upon one of the mountains of which I shall tell you.' So Abraham rose early in the morning, saddled his ass, and took two of his young men with him, and his son Isaac; and he cut the wood for the burnt offering, and arose and went to the place of which God had told him. On the third day Abraham lifted up his eyes and saw the place afar off. Then Abraham said to his young men, `Stay here with the ass; I and the lad will go yonder and worship, and come again to you.' And Abraham took the wood of the burnt offering, and laid it on Isaac his son; and he took in his hand the fire and the knife. So they went both of them together. And Isaac said to his father Abraham, `My father!' And he said, `Here am I, my son.' He said, `Behold, the fire and the wood; but where is the lamb for a burnt offering?' Abraham said, `God will provide himself the lamb for a burnt offering, my son.' So they went both of them together.

"When they came to the place of which God had told him, Abraham built an altar there, and laid the wood in order, and bound Isaac his son, and laid him on the altar, upon the wood.

"Then Abraham put forth his hand, and took the knife to slay his son. But the angel of the Lord called to him from heaven, and said, `Abraham, Abraham!' And he said, `Here am I.' He said, `Do not lay your hand on the lad or do anything to him; for now I know that you fear God, seeing you have not withheld your son, your only son, from me.' And Abraham lifted up his eyes and looked, and behold, behind him was a ram, caught in a thicket by his horns; and Abraham went and took the ram, and offered it up as a burnt offering instead of his son. So Abraham called the name of that place The Lord will provide; as it is said to this day, `On the mount of the Lord it shall be provided.'

"And the angel of the Lord called to Abraham a second time from heaven, and said, `By myself I have sworn, says the Lord, because you have done this, and have not withheld your son, your only son, I will indeed bless you, and I will multiply your descendants as the stars of heaven and as the sand which is on the seashore. And your descendants shall possess the gate of their enemies, and by your descendants shall all the nations of the earth bless themselves, because you have obeyed my voice.'[3]

The Bible doesn't tell us about Sarah's thoughts or feelings in this story, but we can try to imagine how Sarah felt and what she may have said or done. We can retell the story as it might have been told by Sarah. Sarah had the audacity to laugh at God when he said that she would bear a son in her old age. She is also described as a Chaldean princess to whom

Abraham owed his flock, herds, and status. It seems unlikely that such a woman, having borne the longed-for child, would stand by passively as Isaac's father led him off to be sacrificed. Did she suspect what Abraham was up to? What would she have said or done to stop him?

Take some time now to retell the story of Abraham, Sarah and Isaac as Sarah might have told it. Feel free to use poetry, song, dance or other creative ways to tell Sarah's story. Allow yourself plenty of time. In giving a voice to Sarah today we are demanding that our earlier history be acknowledged. that female experience be recognized.

When you have finished, pay attention to your feelings. Do you feel you have been able to give Sarah a voice? Was the process of retelling the story a satisfying one? Dancer and liturgist Fanchon Shur finds great power and satisfaction in the interpretation that Sarah was the "hand of God" that stopped the sacrifice. What is your understanding of the story now?

Carol Ochs, in *The Myth Behind the Sex of God*, discusses the story of Abraham, Isaac and Sarah and finds that in order to prove that Abraham is not rooted in the older tradition, God demands that he renounce the most fundamental tenet of the matriarchal religion and kill his own child. Abraham's choice is between the matriarchal principle of protecting his child and the patriarchal principle of following an abstract ethic, obedience to God. Abraham passes the test and is pronounced fit to be the father of a new, patriarchal religion.[4]

Naomi Goldenberg maintains that giving voice to biblical women cannot save Judaism or the Old Testament for, as she says, "The nature of the religion lies in interplay between a father-God and his Sons. In such a religion, women will always be on the periphery."[5] Some women scholars advocate the complete abandonment of Judaism and Christianity. Others are working to reform these traditions by removing various sexist practices. Goldenberg sees the reformers as engaged in a hopeless effort. She feels that it is futile to defend patriarchal creeds.

Do you agree with Goldenberg that we should abandon Judaism and Christianity, or do you believe that it is possible for these traditions to be meaningful and fulfilling to women today and in future generations? If we abandon them, what may take their place? If we are to reform them, what are some of the ways in which that may happen? What do you think of the approach we have just taken to the Abraham, Sarah, and Isaac story as a way to reform the biblical story so that it includes women? Jot down your responses to these questions.

In a well known old Protestant hymn[6] people sing "We are climbing Jacob's ladder," referring to a Bible story in which Jacob while traveling had a dream in which he saw a ladder reaching to heaven, angels ascending and descending, and God standing above it. Songwriter Carole Etzler took the old tune and changed the words to "We are dancing Sarah's circle." Not only does the song then celebrate a Biblical woman; it also changes the ladder, the hierarchy, of patriarchy into a circle of community.[7]

A minister friend of mine one Sunday set a small step ladder in the front of her church. She gathered the children around her during the service and asked them how you could get two persons on the step ladder at the same time. With some discussion they easily figured out that one person would have to be up and the other down. She reminded them of the old song "We are climbing Jacob's ladder," and said she liked a circle better than a ladder because in a circle no person would be higher than any other person. Then she taught them to sing "We Are Dancing Sarah's Circle." Think about that change as you enjoy your candle.

We are dancing Sarah's circle
We are dancing Sarah's circle
We are dancing Sarah's circle
Sisters one and all.

We will all do our own naming
We will all do our own naming
We will all do our own naming
Sisters one and all.

Here we seek and find our history
Here we seek and find our history
Here we seek and find our history
Sisters one and all.

Every round a generation
Every round a generation
Every round a generation
Sisters one and all.

Birth to death and death to birth now
Birth to death and death to birth now
Birth to death and death to birth now
Sisters one and all.

NINE

Gnostic Christians
as Kindred Spirits

LIGHT YOUR SPECIAL CANDLE and place some fruit juice and a piece of your favorite bread near the candle. Take a few deep breaths and read the following excerpts adapted from a poem by Walt Whitman. The gender of the child has been changed from masculine to feminine.

There was a child went forth every day;
And the first object she look'd upon, that object
    she became:
And that object became part of her for that day,
    or a certain part of the day, or for many years,
    or stretching cycles of years.

The early lilacs became part of this child
And grass, and white and red morning-glories,
    and white and red clover, and the song
    of the phoebe bird,
And the third-month lambs, and the sow's pink-faint
    litter, and the mare's foal, and the cow's calf,
And the noisy brood of the barn-yard, or by the

mire of the pond-side,
And the fish suspending themselves so curiously
   below there—and the beautiful curious liquid,
And the water-plants with their graceful flat
   heads—all became part of her.

Her own parents,
He that had father'd her, and she that had conceiv'd
   her in her womb, and birth'd her,
They gave this child more of themselves than that;
They gave her afterward every day—they became
   part of her.

The blow, the quick loud word, the tight bargain,
   the crafty lure,
The family usages, the language, the company,
   the furniture—the yearning and swelling heart,
Affection that will not be gainsay'd—the sense of
   what is real—the thought if, after all, it
   should prove unreal,
The doubts of day-time and the doubts of night-time,
   the curious whether and how,
Whether that which appears so is so, or is it all
   flashes and specks?
The hurrying tumbling waves, quick-broken crests,
   slapping,
The strata of color'd clouds, the long bar of
   maroon-tint, away solitary by itself—the spread
   of purity it lies motionless in,
The horizon's edge, the flying sea-crow, the fragrance
   of salt marsh and shore mud;
These became part of that child who then went forth
   every day, and who now goes, and will always go
   forth every day.[1]

Whitman suggests that everything we encounter becomes part of us and that we carry all of our experience with us into new situations. It is an especially interesting fact for women to ponder because we carry with us a great variety of specific religious experiences, both positive and negative.

One of the most important tasks we face as women is a sorting of our experiences with religion. We need to clarify what religious values and experiences we wish to bring with us from our earlier lives and what we choose to leave behind. Most of us are clearest about the latter—we are usually very vocal about the religious ideas we want to discard. We tend to forget that there were positive influences in our earlier lives toward freedom of thought and toward the human values we hold now. Those influences may or may not have occurred in churches, but they were religious and we need to honor those experiences and consciously bring them with us into our present search.

As searchers we have another tremendous need, and that is for kindred spirits. We need to know that we are not the only ones to arrive at certain heretical and unorthodox insights. Some of us love to sift through history and claim all the mavericks and heretics as wise women and men who are precursors of our views. It is an important task. It gives us a sense of continuity with unique and creative people of different times.

Think now of your own spiritual quest as a woman and ask yourself the following questions: What values, beliefs, and attitudes from the past do you choose to reject? What belief or value which you have rejected has been the most significant in your life? Take some time now to write down your answers.

Think now of values, beliefs and influences you experienced as positive and ask yourself these questions: What beliefs or values from the past do you choose to retain? What is the most important belief or value you wish to retain? Take time to write down your answers.

In 1945, at a place called Nag Hammadi in Upper Egypt, near a mountain full of caves, a man was digging. When he dug out a boulder he unearthed a large pottery jar. Thinking it might contain gold he smashed it and emptied out the contents. He found no gold but a collection of papyrus books bound in leather. After years of black-market sales, smuggling, and political intrigue, the collection was finally assembled in a museum in Cairo, and copies were made available to scholars. The books have been dated to the fourth century C.E. and identified as copies of scriptures used by Gnostic Christians, some of the very earliest followers of the teachings of Jesus. Their ideas were vehemently attacked and labeled heretical by the growing orthodox Catholic Church, which in that century became the official religion of the Roman Empire. Scholars speculate that someone hid the heretical texts in the hope of reclaiming them later. However they remained safely buried until 1945. As Elaine Pagels points out in *The Gnostic Gospels*, if they had been discovered a thousand years ago, or even a few hundred years ago, surely they would have been burned as heretical.[2]

Among the startling heresies proclaimed by the Gnostic Christians of the fourth century is the notion that humanity created God, and from its own inner potential discovered the revelation of truth. The Greek word gnosis means knowledge. For Gnostics, exploring the psyche became a religious quest. They believed that the psyche bore the potential for liberation or destruction. These words are from the Gospel of Thomas and are attributed to Jesus. He said, "If you bring forth what is within you, what you bring forth will save you. If you do not bring forth what is within you, what you do not bring forth will destroy you." According to the Gnostics, most people live in oblivion and unconsciousness, and so self-knowledge is crucial. In another text Silvanus, a Gnostic teacher said, "Knock on yourself as upon a door and walk upon yourself as a straight road." The Gospel of Truth says, "Say then from the heart that you are the perfect day, and in you dwells the light that does not fail...For you are the understanding that is drawn forth."

Several interesting implications follow from this central focus on self-knowledge. Any person may achieve enlightenment and become her teacher's equal. Authority, then, is derived from self-knowledge and not from one's position in a hierarchy. As Pagels points out, this self-knowledge offers nothing less than a theological justification for refusing to obey the bishops and priests. Gnostic Christians refused to acknowledge the authority of the hierarchy. They operated on a more democratic model by rotating leadership in their churches. A contemporary, Bishop Irenaeus complained that when the Gnostics met, the members first drew lots. Whoever received a certain lot took the role of priest; another acted as bishop; yet another read the Scriptures during worship; and others addressed the group as prophets, offering extemporaneous spiritual instruction. The next time the group met, they drew lots again, so that each person took on different roles. Instead of ranking their members in superior and inferior orders within a hierarchy they followed the principle of perfect equality.

Another implication of the Gnostic view is that since both men and women seek self-knowledge, divinity is visualized in both masculine and feminine terms. Gnostic literature contains such lines as: "I am Thought that dwells in the Light, she who exists before the All, I move in every creature. I am the Invisible One within the All." And this: "I am the first and the last. I am the honored one and the scorned one. I am the whore and the holy one. I am the wife and the virgin, I am the mother and the daughters." The Gnostic Theodotus explained that the saying "according to the image of God he made them, male and female he made them" means that "the male and female elements together constitute the finest production of the Mother Wisdom." As orthodox Christianity rejected female imagery and gradually excluded women from positions of leadership, Gnostic churches continued to encourage female leadership.

Gnostics were severely criticized by the orthodox church fathers. According to Pagels, Bishop Irenaeus noted with dismay that women are especially attracted to heretical groups. He admitted that even in his own district the Gnostic teacher Marcus attracted "many foolish women" from his own congregation including the wife of one of Irenaeus' deacons. Marcus invited women to prophesy and even to act as priests in celebrating the Eucharist. Tertullian expressed similar outrage at the Gnostics. He writes, "These heretical women—how audacious they are! They have no modesty; they are bold enough to teach, to engage in argument, to enact exorcisms, to undertake cures, and, it may be, even to baptize!"

Orthodox Christianity made many theological decisions that strengthened the centralized power of the Church. One of the most crucial and politically ingenious theological decisions had to do with the nature of God. God was determined to be a creator outside the creation rather than within it, except in the person of Jesus. Jesus' resurrection had to be accepted literally because only the apostles were supposed to have seen him after he arose. In this way, only by tracing one's authority through the bishops to the apostles and thus to Jesus, could one have access to God. In case you think this kind of thinking is peculiar to the fourth century, take a look at bumper stickers today that say that Jesus is the one way to God. Gnostics who experienced the divine within themselves and refused to accept a literal interpretation of the resurrection did not really need the bishops or the apostles or even a resurrected Jesus in order to have access to God, so they were labeled heretics.

It may be, as Pagels suggests, that the decisions of the Orthodox Church enabled Christianity to survive. Today, however, it may be that our survival as human beings depends on the assertion of the very principles once espoused by the Gnostic heretics: the freedom to pursue self-knowledge and the use of a democratic process in human relations.

Early Gnostic Christians may be kindred spirits for us as women seeking new—or ancient—spiritual truths. The Gnostics believed that humanity created God, that exploring the psyche is a religious quest, and that self-knowledge is crucial. There are four implications of such a position, each inherently threatening (and thus heretical) to a hierarchal social order:

1. Any person can achieve enlightenment and then become the equal of her teacher.

2. Authority is derived from self-knowledge, not from one's position in a hierarchy. There is no need to obey bishops and priests; leadership is rotated.

3. Both women and men seek self-knowledge, so God is visualized in female as well as male terms, and women and men share equally in leadership.

4. God is within the natural world and in all people, not just in Jesus. There is no need to trace authority back to bishops, apostles, and Jesus in order to gain access to the divine.

Let us turn once again to the passage in the Gospel According to Thomas in which Jesus is quoted as saying, "If you bring forth what is within you, what you bring forth will save you. If you do not bring forth what is within you, what you do not bring forth will destroy you." Jean Baker Miller suggests that if women bring forth their needs, values and priorities, they will find themselves involved in conflict, conflict that is healthy and necessary for growth.[3] As women perhaps we have all felt the beginnings of such conflict when we have asserted ourselves.

To understand the reasons for this inevitable and necessary conflict we need to see that as women we live in a relationship of permanent inequality with men.[4] Permanent in the sense that we are born into a group (women) which is defined by the dominant group (men) as inherently inferior and defective. According to this definition we are allowed or deemed capable of only certain roles and characteristics. Roles which serve the needs of men but are not highly valued or paid; characteristics such as passivity, weakness and nurturing which make us easier to control. Men reserve for themselves the highly paid roles of authority and power, the characteristics of action, intellect and strength.

This unequal relationship with men is considered "normal." For a woman to object to these terms of the relationship is to risk being considered abnormal. It is also to risk economic hardship and social disapproval. In this way the conflict inherent in a relationship of inequality is denied and suppressed by the dominant group. When women assert themselves, they expose the inequality and call into question the whole structure of male-female relationships.

For women, challenging the structures of inequality is a very frightening prospect and that fear is realistic. Self-assertion by a woman in relation to a man—refusing unwanted sexual advances, for example, or just refusing to take his suits to the cleaners—may elicit a severely negative or even a violent response from the man. A woman who acts on her own behalf, by filing a complaint against a man for sexual harassment, or by continuing to work full time outside the home when she has young children, is socially made to feel that she is hurting or depriving others—something she has been carefully taught is wrong. Most destructive of all, she may really believe that she doesn't matter as a person. So completely have we eliminated our own needs and desires from consideration that women are often heard to say "Just for me? If it's just for me, what's the point? That just doesn't seem like any reason at all."[5] To become aware of such an assumption within oneself can be as frightening and depressing as the potential anger of men, or the impossible social imperative to be always giving.

Men have been raised to accept the dominant role in male-female relationships as normal. When an assertive woman objects to that arrangement, men may experience her as irrational or abnormal. They do not see her demands as reasonable or justified. Women often say "He just doesn't get it!" I think of the husband who objected strenuously to his wife's accepting expensive gifts from her parents but secretly accepted thousands of dollars from his own parents in order for him and his wife to buy a house. When his wife found out about this very large gift and objected because he had not even discussed it with her, he accused her of being unreasonable. After all, he just wanted them to be able to buy the house. He was unable to see, much less acknowledge the inequality at the root of her anger.

On an even more absurd level (in my view), another husband refused to allow his wife to do her nails in her own home. He insisted she sit in the garage to paint her nails. When she complained, he insisted it was a reasonable request because nail polish if spilled could harm the finish on their wood furniture. He firmly believed that she was the unreasonable one even though she offered to do her nails in the kitchen or the bathroom. She was unable to assert herself and continued to sit in the garage to paint her nails. She believed him when he said he was just making a reasonable request. She did not believe me when I said it was outrageous.

Other conflicts arise in the business world. A young woman I know was working as a clerk in a drug store. She was asked to take charge of the jewelry and cosmetics department and did extremely well deciding what items to order and keeping careful account of what items sold best. For this added responsibility she was given a very small pay raise but she was pleased to be given the opportunity. Then she discovered that the newly hired male clerk was making almost twice the money that she was and had fewer responsibilities. When she complained, she was met with surprise and was told that the store just could not afford to pay her more at that time but would do so as soon as possible. The issue of the discrepancy between what was paid to men and what was paid to women was evaded, and although she spoke up several more times, the young woman never did get paid at the same level as the male clerk. Eventually she left the job.

These patterns of relationship are changing, but very slowly and only because women have begun to trust their own experience and to speak their own truth. What is the real truth underlying the relationships in your life? Are you able to trust yourself and your perceptions? Do you speak up and take action on your own behalf? What happens when you do?

What conflicts have you experienced when you expressed your newfound strength as a woman? How did you feel? Think carefully of your efforts to assert yourself. Know that you have the right and the power to speak your truth. Know that you have the strength to survive the inevitable conflicts that arise. Eat your special bread; then say aloud "May this bread sustain me in my struggle." Drink your special juice; then say aloud "May the fruits of my effort be sweet."

TEN

Mary

BEFORE YOU BEGIN this chapter, place a few sheets of paper and a pen or pencil alongside your special candle. When you are ready light your candle, breathe deeply and read the following poem:

He came all so stille
   There his mother was
As dew in Aprille
   That falleth on the grass.
He came all so stille
   To his mothers bower
As dew in Aprille
   That falleth on the flower
He came all so stille
   There his mother lay
As dew in Aprille
   That falleth on the spray.
Mother and maiden
   Was never none but she;

well may such a lady
   Goddes mother be.

                    —English carol, 15th century [1]

We begin here to explore the images we have of ourselves as women, the image that has been created of Mary, the Mother of Jesus, and the effects of that Mary image on women past and present.

Consider first the labels you give yourself. On your paper make three columns and label them A, B and C. Write in column A six words or phrases you might use to describe yourself. Now rank those six words or phrases in order of their importance to you. Now write in column B six words or phrases you feel a man might use to describe you. Rank those words and phrases in order of their importance to you. Now write in column C six words or phrases that you think a woman might use to describe you and rank them in order of their importance to you. Look over the lists and the rankings. Are there differences among the three lists? Do you seem to perceive yourself differently from the way you think you are perceived by men? by women?

Do you think that women give themselves labels, or expect labels from others, that imply a subordinate or inferior status? Do we expect such labels more from men than from women? Do the images that are projected in our culture portray women as inferior to men? What are women's expectations or goals for themselves as they enter adulthood versus the realities of today's society? Take some time to write down your responses to these questions.

As human beings we rely heavily upon others for feedback about ourselves and our personal characteristics. The process starts when we are tiny children. The adults in our lives can encourage self-esteem and a positive image of ourselves. They encourage us to speak our first words, take our first steps and they applaud our accomplishments. We learn to trust ourselves and our abilities when we are given that kind of loving encouragement. If we are not affirmed in our attempts to learn, if more attention is paid to our failures than to our successes, if we are belittled rather than made to feel good about ourselves, we will develop a very negative image of ourselves.

Our particular problem as women is that even if we have normally loving families we still receive many messages that define us in negative ways: as less able to succeed at certain tasks, less powerful in becoming independent persons, less ambitious for worldly success. We are applauded for being helpful, caring, pretty, neat, and self-effacing. Boys are applauded, or at least condoned, for being active, messy, aggressive and independent.

There have been many attempts to document the effects of encouragement in the field of education. One widely read study was titled *Pygmalion in the Classroom*.[2] The methodology has been criticized but the hypothesis and some of the results deserve attention. The hypothesis was that the expectations teachers have of particular children will affect the children's achievement, that if teachers are told that children are very bright, the children will perform at a significantly higher level than they otherwise would. According to the results the children's performance increased dramatically when teachers were told children were gifted. It was of course very difficult in such a study to control the many other factors (besides teacher attitudes) that could affect the children's performance. However the statistical tables yielded one very interesting fact. All but one of the statistically significant increases in performance were made by the girls. In other words it was the girls who responded most significantly to the extra encouragement to achieve. The statistical significance of the increase in girls' performance was in fact so great that one has to wonder if there was some validity to the hypothesis despite the methodological shortcomings of the study. And why was it true only for the girls? Do teachers normally give boys plenty of encouragement but fail to do so with girls unless the girls are believed to be especially gifted? The answer is yes.

Other studies have clearly documented the fact that teachers generally call on boys more often and give them more responsibility and encouragement. The teachers do not even realize they are doing so. It is not intentional; it is automatic.

According to Dale Spender in *Invisible Women: The Schooling Scandal*[3], even when teachers think they are being completely fair, the empirical evidence shows that they favor the boys in their classes. Teachers are often surprised when told that they have spent only one third of their class time interacting with the girls. They even say they thought they were spending more time with the girls than the boys.[4] Researchers observed teacher-student interactions and found a pattern that was consistent across all grade levels: boys got more attention than girls and had more intellectual exchanges with teachers.[5] Videotapes of college classes reveal a similar pattern.[6] Men in some classes speak as much as twelve times longer than women, and women are interrupted far more frequently than the men.

As girls and women we are formed and molded by attitudes and behaviors on the part of parents and teachers. Attitudes that unconsciously assume our second class status and abilities. Behaviors that tell us subliminally that we are not as important or as capable as males.

Reading materials quietly reinforce the same messages. In one study eerily entitled *Dick and Jane as Victims*, 134 reading books used in suburban New Jersey public schools were analyzed. The authors write: "From the 2,760 stories we read in 134 books, some startling ratios were derived: boy-centered stories to girl-centered stories, 5:2; adult male main characters to adult female main characters, 3:1; male biographies to female biographies, 6:1; male animal stories to female animal stories, 2:1; male folk or fantasy stories to female folk or fantasy stories, 4:1. Clever girls appear 33 times, clever boys 131 times. Industrious boys 169, industrious girls 47. There are 143 instances of heroic boys, 36 of heroic girls. Nice girls in the stories finish last, are passive, incompetent and put themselves down by saying things like 'I'm just a girl but I know enough not to do that.'"[7]

Until very recently girls and women have suffered a serious lack of role models—women whose independence and accomplishments would tell us that we too had the capacity, the power and the will to do important work in the world. The problem is not that women have not been artists, scientists, political and religious leaders. The problem is that we have not been taught about such women. Or the accomplishments of one particular woman have appeared to us to be an exception to our general understanding that women cannot usually be successful in such endeavors. In general we have been taught to dabble in the arts but not to take our work seriously. As for the sciences and professions other than teaching or nursing, we have been subtly discouraged from even trying.

When we do discover a possible role model, we often assume she must be a special genius whom we could never emulate. In my own life I remember seeing the movie Madame Curie when I was thirteen and returning to see it two more times. Then I read a biography of the great scientist. I was fascinated by the fact that she had married and had two children in addition to her work as a scientist. But I remember thinking at the same time that of course she was a genius and that an ordinary girl like me could not possibly aspire to such a life. I forgot about Marie Curie for many years but the image of a scientist who was also a wife and mother made a deep impression on me. It was an image that emerged from my memory as I juggled the demands of my children and my own desire to go to graduate school. If I had never seen that movie, would I have known that I could do all that? Initially none of the other young mothers I knew were going to graduate school and there were no women in my classes. I felt like a very odd person. It was only as I continued my juggling act that I gradually met a few other women who were doing the same thing. It appalls me that I never learned about Marie Curie in school; only at the movies.

Has our educational system changed? Are girls now presented with many role models? Do they learn about the women who have made enormous contributions to our culture? It had not changed when my daughters were in school in the 70s and 80s. They got tired of their crazy mother always asking them if they were learning about the achievements of women like Marie Curie or Mary Cassatt. "No, Mom. We've never heard of those women." I remember asking if the long struggle for women's suffrage was mentioned in their high school American history classes. It was not. Most recently I visited my granddaughter's elementary school and found that the mural they had painted of Old Stone Age life showed only men! I complained to the teacher. The image my granddaughter is developing of herself as a female human being is at stake! Will she too grow up thinking that only males make the important contributions? How many more generations of women will it take until our educational system provides images of strength and competence and achievement for our daughters?

Let us turn now to the image of Mary in Western religion. What has been your own experience or understanding of Mary? Take a few minutes to write down your experiences and your thoughts about the following questions: What kind of a role model do you think Mary is for women? What labels are given to women because of the image of Mary? Is she Virgin or Mother? Is she passive, or supportive of women's power? What has happened to women as they tried to imitate Mary?

The New Testament scarcely mentions Mary. She is brought into the story mainly to emphasize Jesus's divine conception and birth. Her presence is noted once or twice, but little is made of it. In the centuries that followed, however, Mary was exalted to ever-higher positions of glory.[8] She is the subject of many of our most famous and beautiful works of art. In light of what we have learned about the Goddesses of the ancient Near East, it is interesting that Mary is shown not only as the Madonna with her child, but standing on the crescent moon or with stars circling her head. She takes on many of the ancient Goddess symbols and is often painted as a larger-than-life figure. She is also shown being crowned Queen of Heaven, absorbing the title of the Goddess. It may be that the need of the people for a female deity was so great that the Christian Church might not have survived without the elevation of Mary to this exalted position.[9] We need to look carefully, however, at just what aspects of the Goddess Mary was allowed to retain and what the results were in the lives of women.

Mary was taken up to heaven and seated with god the father and his divine son Jesus. She became the main intercessor between human beings and the divine. She was called Mother of God and Queen of Heaven, but she was not made a full-fledged member of the Godhead. The Church used her to satisfy the need for a female presence in Christianity but also to keep women in a subordinate position. Her purity as a virgin was exalted and women were taught to strive for that purity and to obey the divine (male) will. At the same time she is, of course, a mother, and women were taught to bear as many children as possible. But Mary did it while remaining a virgin; other women, in order to be mothers, must be tainted by sexuality. If they remain pure they cannot be like Mary the Mother; if they become mothers they cannot be like Mary the Virgin. No matter what they do they are guilty and inferior.

Mary's stance is: "Let it be to me according to your word." She is passive, obedient, and pure. She sits on a throne but has little power, certainly none of the power or independence of the earlier Goddesses or their free sexuality. Nevertheless, the doctrine of her virginity gave women a way out of the role of submissive wife and bearer of children. When the cult of Mary was at its height, thousands of women escaped into convents, communities of women. There they developed skills and talents in the arts and in the administration of large estates. Many abbesses wielded significant power and controlled sizable amounts of wealth.[10]

It is interesting that, just as the veneration of Mary reached its height in the fifteenth and sixteenth centuries, the Protestant Reformation reasserted the dominance of the male divinities. One of Luther's major reforms was the closing of nunneries, and Mary is notably absent from all formulations of Protestant theology and ritual. Whereas Catholic women have suffered from their attempts to imitate an impossible model, Protestant women have had no exalted female model of any kind. Mary's presence has been used by the Catholic Church to reinforce the subordination of women, and her absence has been used by Protestantism to reinforce their insignificance.

Consider this comment by Naomi Goldenberg: "It would be far better for women to contemplate the images of the great Goddess behind the myth of Mary than to dwell on the man-made image of Mary herself."[11] Do you agree?

Return now to the words and phrases you wrote about yourself in columns A, B and C. Choose the three qualities you like best in yourself and say them aloud. Know that you have within yourself the power and the will to bring forth these positive qualities in your life. Know that when you do so, other women will be inspired and empowered.

ELEVEN

Witchcraft

BEFORE YOU BEGIN this chapter, place a symbol of the Goddess such as a flower or a spiral shell next to your candle. Add a honey cake or other treat for yourself. Have a large sheet of drawing paper, your crayons and three index cards nearby. As you light your candle say aloud "I light the candle of the Goddess."

Read the following incantation:

Fair Goddess of the rainbow,
Of the stars and of the moon!
The Queen most powerful
of hunters and the night!
We beg of thee thy aid,
That thou may give to us
The best of fortune ever.[1]

As you read the narrative contained in the next six paragraphs pay close attention to your feelings, letting them surface and absorb you.

Some say that when the last Goddess temples were closed, the old Goddess religions went underground and survived in secret as Witchcraft. At first Christianity brought little change because most people saw it as a new version of the Mother Goddess and Her Divine Child who dies and is reborn. Persecution began slowly, but Witchcraft, the religion of the Goddess, was eventually declared heretical, and the full power of Christendom, Church and State, was used to stamp it out. A holocaust of terrifying proportions spread across Europe.

When we speak of Witchcraft, we are speaking of Goddess religion. When we speak of Witchburning we are speaking of the burning of an estimated nine million people, eighty percent of them women. We are speaking of an unspeakable era in women's religious history.

Initially the Witch craze focused on unmarried women, spinsters and widows, and served to rid society of these "unacceptable" groups. Eventually the craze got out of hand, and even the most docile married women were accused. Some villages were left with only one living woman.

Every imaginable torture was used in attempts to obtain confessions and the names of other Witches. One reads of limbs forced asunder, eyes driven out of the head, sinews twisted from the joints, and shoulder blades wrung from the back. The executioner was said to flog with the scourge, crush with screws, load down with weights, stick with needles, burn with brimstone, and singe with torches.

Equally unspeakable was the use and abuse of children. Not only did they watch their mothers being burned alive, but they were often used as legal witnesses against their mothers. Little girls as young as seven were forced to give testimony, which was used to condemn their mothers to death. The burden of self-hatred carried by these daughters has been handed down through the generations to our own time. In Mary Daly's words, "Without knowledge and consent, women are trained to continue the ritual murder of female Divinity, burning the Witch within themselves and each other."[2]

You are a Witch. Think about that! "You are a Witch by being female, untamed, angry, joyous, and immortal."[3]

Now take your paper and crayons and express the feelings you experienced while reading the narrative. Take plenty of time so that all your feelings can be given expression. When you have finished, try to put into a sentence or two what you have tried to show in your drawing. The persecution of Witches is part of your religious history as a woman. How do you feel about that? Is the narrative correct in saying that you are a Witch? Try saying aloud three times "I am a Witch!" How do you feel?

There is only one word in the English language that connotes both women and power. That word is Witch. Consider for a minute that it was not magic or spells that motivated the killing of Witches, but the fear that they might have power—women's power—different and mysterious and uncontrolled by men, the church, or any other hierarchy. Take a few minutes to write your feelings about this.

Modern women, dissatisfied with the image of Mary and the absence of female imagery in contemporary Judaism and Protestantism, are searching intellectually and emotionally for symbols that can express female religious experience. The recent discoveries of archaeological artifacts and writings about the ancient Goddess religion have caught the imagination of women involved in the search for religious symbols.

What happened to the Old Religion when the patriarchal deities came into power? Many women have come to believe that the Old Religion survived in secret as Witchcraft. Christianity was often imposed on the people by a king or ruler who had been converted. To the country people, the pagans (from the Latin *paganus* meaning country person), the new religion seemed familiar: a Mother and Her Divine Child who dies and is reborn. They continued to practice the Old Religion. As the feudal system crumbled however, the stability of the medieval Christian church was shaken and it could tolerate no rivals.

Witchcraft was the religion of the indigenous peoples of Europe, before they were converted, often by force, to Christianity. Witchcraft, or Wicca, as it was called in the Old English language, honored the Great Goddess and Her male consort, the Horned God of the Forests. The Goddess was the power of the Earth and sky, the Moon and the cosmos. The Horned God was the link to the wild things of the Earth, to animals which were hunted for food and to grain, grown and also slain in harvest. The Horned God represented just and willing sacrifice, life taken so that other life may continue.

In 1484 the Papal Bull of Innocent VII turned the Inquisition against the Old Religion. The *Malleus Malleficarum*, or *Hammer of the Witches*, was published in 1486, and a reign of terror began which lasted into the eighteenth century in Europe. "All Witchcraft stems from carnal lust which in women is insatiable," stated the *Malleus Malleficarum.* Every unspeakable torture was inflicted to obtain "confessions." The Old Religion of the Goddess was driven underground, passed down in a few, isolated families. By the time the persecutions ended only hideous stereotypes remained—Witches as evil, ugly hags, laughable to modern people. The Horned God, with his antlers and cloven hooves, symbol of the Earth and lover of the Goddess, became the Christian devil.

Today as women seek new ways to express their spiritual feelings the Goddess symbol has re-emerged and has inspired us "to see ourselves as Divine, our bodies as sacred, the changing phases of our lives as holy, our aggression as healthy, our anger as purifying, and our power to nurture and create, but also to limit and destroy as necessary, as the very force that sustains all life."[4]

Starhawk points out that the symbolism of the Goddess is not parallel to the symbolism of God the Father. "The Goddess does not rule the world; She *is* the world."[5] She is manifest in each of us and can be known by every person. In Witchcraft each person must reveal her or his own truth. Sexuality is sacred. Religion is a matter of relinking with the Divine within, and with the Divine in all the human and natural world.

The patriarchal images of God as outside nature and of man as having dominion over the Earth have allowed us to exploit and destroy nature. Pollution and ecological destruction have resulted. Witchcraft is a religion of ecology that recognizes the sacred interdependence of all living things.

The symbols of the Goddess and Witchcraft appeal to men too. It allows them to experience and to integrate in themselves qualities usually called feminine. In addition, many men who are concerned about the fate of the Earth are drawn to Witchcraft and the Goddess because of its strong emphasis upon the sacredness of all life. They wish to adopt an attitude of harmony with rather than dominion over the Earth. The Goddess's consort, the Horned One, was a God and steward of the Earth and His symbolism is also a very rich tradition in which men may discover the Sacred.

The ethics of Witchcraft are based on the concept of the Goddess as immanent in all forms of life, human beings, and all the Earth's plants and creatures, even the living processes of biospheres. Love for life is the basic ethic, and Witches are bound to honor and respect all living things. Justice is seen as an understanding that each act brings about consequences that must be faced responsibly. The rule is "Do as you will so long as you harm no one." What is cultivated is an inner sense of pride and self-respect. No one has the right to coerce another.

Witchcraft today is a new religion and its philosophy contains some important ideas for us to consider. First, Witches believe the Divine is internalized as the Goddess or God within each of us, and so each person is responsible for her or his own beliefs and behavior. Secondly, like Gnostic Christians, Witches believe in a democratic process of shared leadership. Thirdly, the Divine is imagined as immanent in all of life, so Witchcraft is vitally concerned about the well-being of the Earth.

Immanence is a form of consciousness that perceives everything in the world as being alive and imbued with the life energy of the Divine. Everything is living in an interdependent web. Everything has value, and not the kind of value capitalism places on objects. Everything has value simply because it is, because it is a part of the Divine.

All natural objects then, have spirit, just as do people. Trees, grass, birds, animals. The sacred groves in which pagans and witches met to worship were embodiments of the Spirit of nature and were honored. Judaism and Christianity saw this as idolatrous. They declared Nature to be dead, inanimate and subject to domination. The same attitude was held about women, who for many years were said not to have souls. Witchcraft is a religion that sees all of creation as having souls, and the four elements that make up creation—Air Fire, Water and Earth—as the four most sacred things. Starhawk writes:

> The Earth is a living, conscious being. In company with cultures of many different times and places, we name these things as sacred: Air, Fire, Water and Earth.
>
> Whether we see them as the Breath, Energy, Blood and Body of the Mother, or as the blessed gifts of a Creator, or as symbols of the interconnected systems that sustain life, we know that nothing can live without them.
>
> To call these things sacred is to day that they have a value beyond their usefulness for human ends, that they themselves become the standards by which our laws and purposes must be judged. No one has the right to appropriate them or profit from them at the expense of others. Any government which fails to protect them forfeits its legitmacy.
>
> All people, all living things, are part of the Earth-life, and so sacred. No one stands higher or lower than any other. Only justice can assure balance; only ecological balance can sustain freedom. Only in freedom can that fifth sacred thing we call Spirit flourish in its full diversity.
>
> To honor the sacred is to create conditions in which nourishment, sustenance, habitat, knowledge, freedom and beauty can thrive. To honor the sacred is to make love possible.

To this we dedicate our curiousity, our will, our courage, our silences, and our voices. To this we dedicate our lives.[6]

As women explore the Divine within ourselves and within all of nature we begin to feel the need for ritual, the ceremonial observance of events in our lives. Ritual is a way of looking at the experiences we have, ascribing special meaning to certain moments or events, and celebrating these meanings with people close to us. Ritual is also a way of getting in touch with our own deepest joys and sorrows, and with the power and the will within us that can heal and can enable us to act on behalf of ourselves and our values. Ritual in that sense is very political. Once we are aware of our own situation as women in a patriarchal society, and of the ecological crisis facing the sacred Earth, there is no turning back. Our eyes have been opened and the only road we can travel with integrity is the road of action: action to empower women; action to preserve the Earth. It is not an easy road. In one of her songs Carol Etzler sings "Sometimes I wish my eyes hadn't been opened. Sometimes I wish I could no longer see all of the pain and the hurt and the longing of my sisters and me as we try to be free..."[7]

Ritual in community with others is a way to empower ourselves for the inevitable conflicts we face as women who would honor ourselves and the Earth.

To begin a ritual we create a sacred space where we can feel safe and can allow ourselves to be in touch with the deepest levels of our consciousness. Groups often create such a space by forming or casting a Circle. One person may walk around the entire Circle, or the group may simply join hands to mark the space.

Because we wish to invoke our fullest deepest selves, we often invoke the Goddess within each of us by lighting a special candle and saying something like "Maiden, Mother,

Crone, Light of the world which is yourself...See with our eyes, hear with our ears, touch with our hands, breathe with our nostrils, kiss with our lips, open our hearts. Come into us! Touch us, change us, make us whole."[8] If men are present we may also invoke the God within. Because we long to be in harmony with the natural world we often light a candle at each of the four directions and call upon their powers to be with us:

East represents the element of Air and the powers of intellect and new beginnings.

South represents the element of Fire and the powers of passion and energy.

West represents the element of Water and the powers of intuition and stillness.

North represents the element of Earth and the powers of our physical bodies, manifestation and groundedness.

In the center of the circle we often have another special candle for the central point of transformation or change, a focus for meditations which call us to inner change.

Rituals are often done at the time of natural events such as the Winter and Summer Solstices, Spring and Fall Equinoxes, or the Full Moon or New Moon each month. Usually some analogy is made with our personal lives. At the time of the Winter Solstice, for example, we may meditate upon the night of longest darkness as a time to look within for the wishes, the new projects, the parts of ourselves we wish to bring forth into the light. In one such ritual each person brought a candle and at a certain point each was asked to think of what they wished to bring forth and then to light the candle and place it on an altar in the center of the Circle. As all the individual candles were lighted the whole room brightened and each person was told by the group "You have your wish."

Sometimes rituals are planned to celebrate a transition, a new learning or the special desire of a particular person. If you are out of work and struggling to keep up your self-confidence in the face of repeated rejections it can be very helpful to gather your community of trusted friends for a ritual. Such a ritual can reassure you of your abilities, build up your confidence and make you aware of the caring and encouragement of your friends.

For many women it has been important to create positive rituals for their daughters on the occasion of their first menstruation. For some of us it has been exhilarating to celebrate menopause with a special ritual as a time of entering into our wisdom and power as older women.

For women and men who care deeply about the fate of the Earth it has been empowering to enact rituals at demonstrations against nuclear power and other forms of damage to the environment.

Women who create rituals often speak of energy or power being raised by drumming or chanting or dancing. Participating in these activities in the context of ritual which has a special focus can indeed evoke in us a sense of confidence and power and excitement about our job search, our transition to a new phase of life, or the light and hope of our new awareness. Most importantly, such energy empowers us to act in ways that enhance our lives and give voice to our deepest convictions.

When the ritual is ended we thank the elements of nature represented by the four directions for their presence and we thank the Divine within each person for Her or His presence. We open the circle by saying "The Circle is open but unbroken. May the peace of the Goddess go in your hearts, merry meet and merry part and merry meet again. Blessed be!"[9]

Like any religion, Witchcraft has developed some special symbols which all Witches will recognize and use in ritual or meditation. One of the most revered symbols is the pentacle, or five-pointed star. Like any good and long-lasting symbol it has generated many interpretations. Sometimes it represents the human body with its four limbs and head; sometimes the five senses; sometimes the four elements of Air Fire, Water and Earth plus the fifth sacred thing, which is spirit, essence or transformation. The five points of the pentacle can also represent the five stages of live—birth, initiation, love, advanced age and death. Sometimes the five points are used to represent principles such as selfhood, passions, pride, power and wisdom.

The pentagram, or drawing of the pentacle, is often used by individuals for private meditation. To get a feeling for the rituals and meditations of Witchcraft, draw your own pentagrams on your cards. Let them represent you—your head, arms, and legs on one; your five senses on another; and the five stages of your life on the third. Label each point of the pentagram with these words as you see in the illustrations, but remember that the ones you have drawn represent your life. You may add personal notes or memories on your personal pentagrams. When you have the three pentagrams ready, read the following meditation:

Sit comfortably now and hold your first and second personal pentagrams in your hands. Breathe deeply and feel the natural power of your body. Be aware of the muscles of your legs and feet which carry you every day. Be aware next of your arms and hands and the miracle of your fingers and your sense of touch. Now

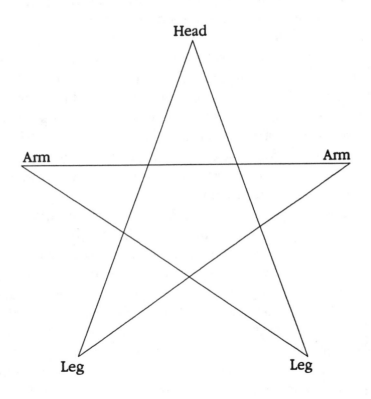

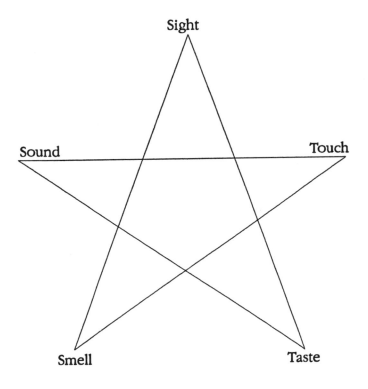

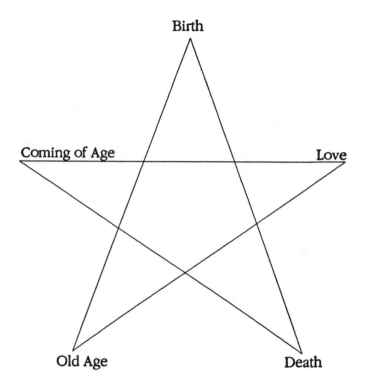

notice your head and be aware of the wonders of your brain, your eyes, ears, sense of smell and taste. Take your time and give each your attention. If you are impaired in any of your limbs or senses, notice the increased sensitivity and ability you have developed in the others.

Now hold your third pentagram and let yourself move into your memories of early infancy and childhood. Take your time and reclaim some of the sights, sounds, smells and tastes of your early life. When you are ready, imagine yourself as you began to grow into an adult. What were the hopes, the ideals that guided you? See yourself as a young adult and remember your first love. Be aware of the sacred power of your sexuality. Ponder also the responsibilities of your adult life. Be aware of the directions your life has taken. Are they satisfying? Think now of yourself as an old woman, full of the wisdom and power that has grown out of your life's experiences. When the time comes, will you be ready to let go, to allow your life to end, to feel that it was good?

Return now to your present life and its satisfactions, its frustrations, and your hopes for its future. Feel again the natural power of your own body, your own mind and your own feelings. Let that power and the energy of the Earth flow through you and return to the Earth. Let it bless and inform your life this very day.

Contemporary women in search of new religious symbols have created a new religion in modern Witchcraft utilizing aspects of ancient Goddess spirituality. They use religion and ritual to build personal strengths, and they practice a religion that places Divinity within the person. Whatever may have been the beliefs of Witches in the past, the Witches of today are creating a powerful new religion. In that religion a woman's worth and dignity at all ages are reinforced.

Take some time now to eat your special treat and to write in your journal your feelings about the meditation and about some of the ideas expressed here about Witchcraft.

TWELVE

Future Fantasies

BEFORE YOU BEGIN this chapter get yourself a large piece of craft paper, some old magazines with lots of pictures, scissors and some glue. When you are ready, light your candle, breathe deeply and allow yourself to enter into this fantasy about your future:

It is fifteen years in the future and a special event is being held in your honor. See yourself on that special day. Look around you. Where is the event being held? Who is there? What are you being honored for? How do you feel about the honor? Stay for some moments with your images of the event—the setting, the people, the honor.

Take time now to write the fantasy in your journal along with your thoughts and feelings about it.

What does the fantasy tell you about your hopes for yourself and your future? Does the fantasy represent in some way a real goal in your life? What can you do today to move toward that goal? What changes do you need to make in yourself to reach your goal? What changes do you need to make in your surroundings, your work, your relationships? Where can you find the confidence and the emotional support to move ahead on your journey? Take some time to write down your responses.

Consider now the future of various institutions in our society. Which of our institutions do you encounter in your daily life? How would you change these institutions, such as families, schools, religion, businesses, government, so that girls and boys, women and men will receive equal respect and opportunity within each? What can you personally do to effect change in one or more of these institutions?

Take some time now to create a collage of the changes you would like to see in one of our institutions. Cut pictures from magazines and paste them onto a large sheet of craft paper to express your images of change.

One of the most important learnings to emerge from the women's movement is that the personal is political. If women told the truth about their personal lives and acted on that truth, the very foundations of our patriarchal society would tremble. Elizabeth Oakes Smith said it at a women's rights convention in 1852: "My friends, do we realize for what purpose we are convened? Do we fully understand that we aim at nothing less than an entire subversion of the present order of society, a dissolution of the whole existing social compact?"[1]

Riane Eisler, in her book, *The Chalice and the Blade: Our History, Our Future,* has suggested that there are basically two ways to organize society. We can use a partnership model or a dominator model.[2] We are accustomed to the dominator model and can barely even visualize the partnership model. The dominator model exists where one group (males) rules and another group (females) obeys. Such a model generalizes to all kinds of relationships such as white over black and rich over poor. Power is defined as power over others, as the ability to control them. Institutions using this model have hierarchies. Our religious mythology, for example, has God at the top, the angels just below, then man, then woman, then children and at the very bottom, the Earth and its creatures. Churches such as the Roman Catholic have a pope, below him the cardinals, below them the bishops, below them the priests, below them the people. In such an organization authority or power comes from the top down. Schools and businesses have their own hierarchies. So does the patriarchal family. Someone always rules over someone else.

What about our government which is supposed to be a representative democracy? We have seen that it has not been truly representative but has painstakingly, often grudgingly, moved toward that ideal, granting the vote to more and more people and interpreting the constitution in ever more inclusive ways. The people in power, however, are still overwhelmingly male and overwhelmingly white. Many dominator attitudes persist and inform the way government bureaucracies operate. Yet I believe we do have a form of government that could incorporate more and more egalitarian or partnership ways.

Do we know what a partnership society would be like? Partnership not only between men and women but among races and species? Certainly not in any detail, but we can put forth some basic ideas about necessary changes.

Perhaps the most basic change we need to make is to abandon the destructive dualism which pervades our thinking. We tend to divide the world into we and they, good and evil, friends and enemies. We know that no individual or group is all good or all bad but we persist in this type of thinking. Those who belong to the dominator group see others as different, less important, or in the case of an institution like slavery as not even human. Different, less important and non-human are often easily translated to bad or evil. The oppressed seeth with resentment which cannot be expressed directly but can often be channeled by the dominant group into hatred for other groups or nations.

We need to climb down from our various ladders of hierarchy and try respecting each other as equals in worth and dignity. Men who have been giving the orders need to stop and learn how to listen to the stories, the needs, the valuable ideas of women. White men and women who have assumed much power over men and women of color need to stop and learn how to listen to the stories, the needs, the valuable ideas of their brothers and sisters of color. Those of us who have been oppressed and have turned the anger inward, blaming and degrading ourselves, need to learn how to speak up, to make ourselves and our ideas heard. Listen. Speak. When we do there will be anger. Respect it. Given the many centuries of we/they thinking, perhaps there will be anger for a very long time. We have to look beneath the anger for some positive and universal basis for trust and communication. To abandon the dualism means to acknowledge that we are all in this life and on this planet together.

Another necessary change is toward the building of consensus and away from self-righteous confrontation. We do need to confront each other with our needs, hopes, and ideals across all the old barriers. But just to confront is not to find resolution. We need to redefine power as strength from within. We need to learn how to negotiate, to build consensus, in our personal lives and as a nation in our dealings with other nations. To build consensus is to let go of the idea that any one person or group has the whole truth. To move away from self-righteousness is to open ourselves to a more complete perspective.

If we can make these two basic changes in attitude and behavior, abandoning the we/they dualism and learning to build consensus, we will be much better equipped to find creative ways to move all of our institutions toward the partnership model. Moving toward partnership means moving toward peace. Peace that is not just the absence of war but a condition of equal justice for all people and respect for the sacredness of the Earth.

What will religion be like in a partnership society? The Great Goddess of old has been rediscovered within ourselves and within the whole of nature. Women have tapped the roots of their own worth and power. Men are seeing the importance of reclaiming the sacredness of the Earth. New myths and symbols will emerge as we move toward a partnership model in our institutions. One image has already appeared and seems to be gaining in popularity—the photograph of our Earth taken from space. It is at once an achievement of our most modern science and a stunning and beautiful picture of our ancient home. We await the epic story, the great myth of how human beings, female and male, learned to value and respect each other and the planet.

The story begins with you as you look within for the power to change the patterns and the assumptions of your own life. In the Yoruba religion of Africa, personal power, *ashe*, is personified in a variety of *orishas*, or deities. Yemaya is the Mother of the Sea, the Great Water, the Womb of Creation.

Yemaya gazes often into the waters. Each time she wonders who that beautiful woman is who stares back at her. One time as she wondered her belly grew until it exploded, covering the land with lakes and rivers and streams. Then Yemaya looked into the waters again, and wondered about the beautiful woman she saw. Again her belly grew until it exploded and filled the heavens with stars and a full moon. Finally Yemaya looked into the full moon and even there she saw that same beautiful woman. Once again her belly grew until it exploded and there before her stood thousands of beautiful women. "Who are you beautiful women?" Yemaya asked. The women looked deep into the eyes of the Goddess Yemaya and there they saw their own reflections. So the women said to Yemaya "We're you."[3]

Blessed be!

APPENDIX

IF YOU WISH TO CONTINUE your spiritual journey there are many books for you to read. Some of the most basic and popular books are listed in the bibliography for this book, but there are many new ones published each year. Women scholars are exploring in depth all the areas touched on in the chapters of this book.

If reading alone doesn't seem like enough for your journey, gather a few close friends around you on a regular basis (once a week or once a month) and share your responses to the books you are reading. Encourage your friends to bring their special candles or Goddess images and decorate a small table in your livingroom or wherever you meet. Add a flower, a shell or a pretty rock and enjoy the arrangement as you talk. Take turns providing a special treat to eat or drink. Give yourselves the gifts of time, of intellect, of friendship and food and drink. Remind each other that you each deserve these special moments for exploring the meaning of your lives and your own religious history as women.

Perhaps you and your friends will wish to do more than discuss your reading. You could celebrate the Earth and its seasons, the sun, moon and stars and their movements. Some women meet on the night of each new moon to mark a series of new beginnings in their lives. You might wish to celebrate the return of the sunlight at the Winter Solstice by lighting many candles or by exchanging small gifts. You could meet at the time of the Spring and Fall Equinox, when light and darkness are equal, to explore the meaning of balance in your lives.

Perhaps your friends would also like to gather in celebration of events in your personal lives: the birth of a child, first menstruation of a daughter, your own arrival at menopause, a new job, a major risk like ending a relationship or beginning a new one. Perhaps one of you will need to grieve from time to time. Use your own needs and imaginations. Do what seems meaningful to you.

For your rituals or celebrations make use of all your senses. Use colors that fit the occasion or the season. Begin to collect candles of various sizes and colors. As you learn the stories of various Goddesses, tell them when they fit the occasion. Acquire or make Goddess images to use at different times. Experiment with various kinds of incense. Learn some chants or songs to sing. Get to know some of the meditative music women have composed. Try some simple movements to music, moving in a circle or spiraling together for example. Celebrate with your whole body, your whole self, on each occasion. Use joyous color, music, movement for happy occasions; use quiet reflective poetry, music or colors for sad occasions.

Now gather together, draw strength from each other and celebrate your lives and your creativity.

Notes

Preface

1. Shirley Ann Ranck, *Cakes for the Queen of Heaven.* (Boston: Unitarian Universalist Association, 1986).
2. Carol Christ. "Why Women Need the Goddess," *Heresies* (Spring 1978): 8-12.

Introduction

1. Simone de Beauvoir, *The Second Sex.* (New York, Bantam Books, 1961): xix.
2. H.R. Trevor-Roper, "The European Witch-Craze and Social Change," *Witchcraft and Sorcery*, Max Merxick, ed. (Harmondsworth, England: Penguin Books, 1970).
3. Luisah Teish, "Multicolored Momma," in *Jambalaya.* (San Francisco: Harper & Row, 1985): 89-90.
4. Raphael Patai, *The Hebrew Goddess.* (Hoboken, NJ: KTAV Publishing House Inc. 1967).
5. Harry Emerson Fosdick, *A Guide to Understanding the Bible.* (New York, Harper & Bros., 1938): Chapter 1.

6. Ernst Troeltsch, *The Social Teaching of the Christian Churches*, O. Wyon., trans. (New York, Harper & Row, 1960).

7. Naomi Goldenberg, *The Changing of the Gods*. (Boston, Beacon Press, 1979), Chapter 4.

8. Thealogy is a word coined by Naomi Goldenberg. In Greek, *theos* means god, (male) and *thea* means goddess. Hence, theology (study of god) and thealogy (study of Goddess).

9. For a brilliant and terrifying explication of the devastating effects of the separation of humanity from nature, see Al Gore, *Earth in the Balance: Ecology and the Human Spirit.* (New York: Houghton Mifflin Company, 1992).

10. Elizabeth Cady Stanton, *The Original Feminist Attack on the Bible.* (New York, Arno Press, 1974): 11.

11. Ibid., 11.

12. Elaine Pagels, *The Gnostic Gospels.* (New York, Random House, 1979).

Chapter 1

1. Ellen Bass, "First Menstruation," in *Tangled Vines*, Lyn Lifshin, ed. (Boston: Beacon Press, 1979): 58.

2. Charlene Spretnak, *Lost Goddesses of Early Greece.* (Boston: Beacon Press, 1981): 45.

3. For a more detailed poetic telling of this myth see Spretnak, op. cit., 47-49.

4. Joseph Campbell, *The Masks of God: Primitive Mythology.* (New York: Penguin Books, 1976), 313.

5. Marija Gimbutas, *The Language of the Goddess.* (San Francisco: Harper & Row, 1989): 316.

6. Ibid., p. 316.

7. Karen Horney, *Feminine Psychology.* (New York: W. W. Norton & Co. Inc., 1967): 60-61.

8. Inge K. Broverman et al., "Sex Role Stereotypes and Clinical Judgments of Mental Health." *Journal of Consulting and Clinical Psychology* 34 (1970): 1-7.

9. Joseph Campbell, *The Masks of God: Occidental Mythology.* (New York: Viking-Penguin, Inc., 1964): 315.

10. Campbell, *Masks of the Gods, Primitive Mythology*, 313.

11. Ntosake Shange, *For Colored Girls Who Have Considered Suicide When the Rainbow is Enuf.* (New York: Bantam Books, 1980): 67.

Chapter 2

1. Monica Sjoo and Barbara Mor, *The Great Cosmic Mother.* (San Francisco: Harper & Row, 1987): 10.

2. Ibid., p. 187.

3. G. Rachel Levy, *The Gate of Horn.* (London: Faber & Faber Ltd. 1948.) Quoted in Sjoo and Mor, ibid., 8.

4. Marija Gimbutas, *The Language of the Goddess*, 316-317.

5. Levy, *The Gate of Horn*, 8.

6. Sjoo and Mor, *The Great Cosmic Mother*, 8.

7. Fran P. Hosken, *Women's International Network News* 2, No. 1 (Jan. 1976): 30-44. Quoted in Sjoo and Mor, *The Great Cosmic Mother*, 5.

8. Stephen J. Gould, *Hen's Teeth and Horse's Toes: Reflections in Natural History.* (New York: W. W. Norton, 1983): 153-54.

9. Mary Jane Sherfey, *The Nature and Evolution of Female Sexuality.* (New York: Vintage Books, 1973) 43.

10. Sjoo and Mor, *The Great Cosmic Mother*, 4-5.

11. Patricia Aburdeen and John Naisbitt, *Megatrends for Women.* (New York: Villard Books, 1992): 134.

12. Ibid., 134.

13. Ibid. p., 135.

14. Ibid., p. 143.

15. Ibid., p. 144.

16. Ibid., p. 135-36.

17. Mary Daly, *Gyn/Ecology*. (Boston: Beacon Press, 1978): Chapter 7.

18. Judy Small, "The IPD," from the album *One Voice in the Crowd* 1985, Plaza PZ 006 (distributed by CBS) Released in the U.S.A. by Redwood Records (RR 8503).

19. This discussion including quotes from Church Fathers is based upon Barbara G. Walker, *The Woman's Encyclopedia of Myths and Secrets*. (San Francisco: Harper & Row, 1983): 921.

20. For a more comprehensive telling of this story see Merlin Stone, *Ancient Mirrors of Womanhood*. (Boston: Beacon Press, 1991): 444-45.

21. This discussion is based upon Sjoo and Mor, *The Great Cosmic Mother*, 158-59.

Chapter 3

1. Mary Daly, *Beyond God the Father*. (Boston: Beacon Press, 1973): 13.

2. Jean Baker Miller, *Toward a New Psychology of Women*. (Boston: Beacon Press, 1976): Chapter 10.

3. W. W. Hallo and J.A.A. Van Dijk, trans., "Nin-Me-Sar-Ra," in *The Exaltation of Inanna*. (New Haven: Yale University Press, 1968) 15-35.

Chapter 4

1. Barbara Walker, *The Woman's Encyclopedia of Myths and Secrets*. (San Francisco: Harper & Row, 1983): 667.

2. Quoted in Ariel Salleh, "Living With Nature: Reciprocity or Control?" in J. R. Engel and J. G. Engel, *Ethics of Environment and Development*. (Tucson: University of Arizona Press, 1990):

3. Michael Phillips and Salli Rasberry. *The Seven Laws of Money Word* Wheel and Random House, New York, 1974, Chapter 7.

4. Patricia Aburdeen and John Naisbitt, *Megatrends for Women*, Chapter 3.

5. Phillips, op. cit. Chapter 1

6. Aburdeen & Naisbitt, op, cit. Chapter 3.

7. Excerpted from Luisah Teish, *Jambalaya*, 120-121.

Chapter 5

1. Ellen Bass, "For My Mother," in *Tangled Vines*, Lyn Lifshin, ed. (Boston: Beacon Press, 1979): 36-42.

2. Sojourner Truth, Women's Rights Convention, Akron, Ohio, 1851. Quoted in Patricia C. McKissack and Frederick McKissack *Sojourner Truth: Ain't I a Woman?* (Scholastic Inc., New York, 1992, 112-114.)

3. Marge Piercy, "My Mother's Novel," in Tangled Vines, 43.

4. For a more detailed and poetic version of this myth, see Charlene Spretnak, *Lost Goddesses of Early Greece*, 109-118.

5. Ibid. 105-107.

6. Barbara Walker, *The Crone*. Harper & Row, San Francisco, 1985, p. 12.

Chapter 6

1. Marge Piercy, "A Work of Artifice" in *Circles on the Water*, Alfred A. Knopf Inc. 1982.

2. Mary Daly, "Enuma elish," in *Gyn/Ecology*, 107.

3. For a more detailed and poetic version of this myth, see Spretnak, *Lost Goddesses of Early Greece*, 99-101.

4. Johann Jakob Bachofen, *Myth, Religion and Mother Right* Ralph Manheim, trans. Princeton: Bolingen Series, Princeton University Press, 1967. This volume is a translation of *Mutterrecht und Urreligion*, a selection of the writings of J.J.

Bachofen first published in 1926 by Alfred Kroner Verlag, Stuttgart.

5. Riane Eisler, *The Chalice and the Blade: Our History, Our Future.* Harper & Row, San Francisco, 1987, Chapter 2.

6. Erich Neumann, *The Great Mother.* (Princeton: Bollingen Series, Princeton University Press, 1972).

7. Spretnak, op. cit., 17-38.

8. Naomi Goldenberg, *Changing of the Gods.* (Boston: Beacon Press, 1979), Chapter 5.

9. Merlin Stone, *When God Was a Woman.* (New York: Dial Press, 1976), Chapter 4.

10. Miller, *Toward a New Psychology of Women*, 128.

11. Starhawk, *The Spiral Dance: The Rebirth of the Religion of the Great Goddess*, 2nd edition. (San Francisco, Harper and Row, 1989) 76-77.

Chapter 7

1. Raphael Patai, *The Hebrew Goddess.* (New York: KTAV Publishing House, 1967).

2. Goldenberg, *Changing of the Gods*, Chapter 4.

3. Theo Wells, "Woman—Which Includes Man of Course: An Experience in Awareness." *Newsletter for Humanistic Psychology*, Dec. 1970.

4. Patai, op. cit., p. 8-9.

5. Bible, Revised Standard Version, Jeremiah 7:17-18.

6. Jeremiah 44: 16-18.

7. Goldenberg, op. cit. p. 3-4.

Chapter 8

1. Wittig, *Les Guerilleres.* (Boston: Beacon Press, 1985) 89.

2. Printed by permission of Elinor Artman. Published in the *Journal of Women and Religion*, Center for Women and

Religion, Graduate Theological Union, Berkeley, CA, Vol. I, No. 1, Spring 1981.

3. Bible, Revised Standard Version, Genesis 22:1-18.

4. Carol Ochs, *The Myth Behind the Sex of God.* (Boston, Beacon Press, 1977): 44-45.

5. Goldenberg, *Changing of the Gods*, 7.

6. For the complete text and music of this hymn, see *The United Methodist Hymnal*, The United Methodist Publishing House, Nashville, TN, 1989, #418.

7. Carol Etzler, from the album *Sometimes I Wish*, Samray Music/Sisters Unlimited 1976.

Chapter 9

1. Excerpted and adapted from the poem by Walt Whitman from *Leaves of Grass.* (New York: Heritage Press Edition) 328-330.

2. This discussion, including quotes from Gnostic sources and Church Fathers, is based upon Elaine Pagels, *The Gnostic Gospels.*

3. Miller, *Toward a New Psychology of Women*, Chapter 11.

4. This discussion is based upon Miller, op. cit., Chapter 1.

5. Ibid., p. 122.

Chapter 10

1. Quoted in Marina Warner, *Alone of All Her Sex*, New York, Simon & Schuster, 1976.

2. R. Rosenthal and L. Jacobson, *Pygmalion in the Classroom.* (New York: Holt, Rinehart & Winston Inc., 1968)

3. Dale Spender, *Invisible Women: The Schooling Scandal.* (London: Writers and Readers Publishing, 1982).

4. For an excellent summary of this research, see "Girls Talk; Boys Talk More." *The Harvard Education Letter*, Vol. 7 No. 1, (Jan/Feb 1991).

5. Myra Sadker and David Sadker, "Sexism in the Classroom of the 80s." *Psychology Today*, March 1986.

6. Catherine Krupnick, "Women and Men in the Classroom: Inequality and Its Remedies." *On Teaching and Learning: Journal of the Harvard Danforth Center*, Spring 1985.

7. *Dick and Jane as Victims*, (Princeton: Women on Words & Images, 1972), 8-24.

8. This discussion is based upon Marina Warner, *Alone of All Her Sex*. (New York:Simon & Schuster, 1976).

9. For further discussion of the exaltation of Mary, see Geoffrey Ashe, *The Virgin*. (London: Routledge & Kegan Paul, 1976).

10. For more information on this phenomenon, see Joan Morris, *The Lady Was a Bishop*. (New York: Macmillan, 1973).

11. Goldenberg, *Changing of the Gods*, 76.

Chapter 11

1. This incantation was used by women witches in Tuscany. These women claimed to be of a "family tradition" unbroken since time immemorial. Charles G. Leland met and became friends with one of the Italian *strega*, who shared with him much of her lore, which he translated and published as *Aradia, Gospel of the Witches*. (reprinted by Phoenix Publishing, Inc. of Custer, WA). It is a very curious volume, as it shows both how a witchcraft tradition survived, and how it became corrupted by isolation and Christian influence into a religion of almost pure rebellion.

2. Daly, *Gyn/Ecology*, 197.

3. Robin Morgan, ed., *Sisterhood is Powerful*. (New York: Random House, 1970): 540.

4. Starhawk, *The Spiral Dance*, 9.

5. Ibid., 9.

6. Starhawk, "Declaration of the Four Sacred Things." From *The Fifth Sacred Thing*, New York, Bantam Books, 1993.

7. Carol A. Etzler, *Sometimes I Wish*, Samray Music/Sisters Unlimited, 1976.

8. Starhawk, op. cit. p. 86-87.

9. For a detailed and very beautiful explanation of witchcraft ritual, see Starhawk, op. cit.

Chapter 12

1. Quoted in Daly, *Beyond God the Father*, 155.

2. Riane Eisler, *The Chalice and the Blade*.

3. For a more detailed and dramatic telling of this story, see Teish, *Jambalaya*, 118-19.

Bibliography

Abel, Elizabeth and Emily K. Abel, eds. *The Signs Reader: Women, Gender and Scholarship.* Chicago: University of Chicago Press, 1983.

Aburdeen, Patricia and John Naisbitt, *Megatrends for Women.* New York: Villard Books, 1992.

Adler, Margo. *Drawing Down the Moon: Witches, Druids, Goddess-Worshipers and Other Pagans in America Today.* Revised and expanded edition. Boston: Beacon Press, 1986.

Allen, Paula Gunn. *The Sacred Hoop,* Beacon Press, Boston, 1986.

Artman, Elinor. "Between Two Gods." *Journal of Women and Religion,* Volume 1, Number 1. Berkeley, CA: Center for Women and Religion, Graduate Theological Union, Spring, 1981.

Ashe, Geoffrey. *The Virgin.* London: Routledge and Kegan Paul, 1976.

Austen, Hallie Iglehart. *The Heart of the Goddess.* Berkeley, CA: Wingbow Press, 1990.

Bachofen, Jacob. *Myth, Religion and Mother Right.* Bolligen series LXXIV. Princeton, NJ: Princeton University Press, 1967.

Berger, Pamela. *The Goddess Obscured.* Boston: Beacon Press, 1985.

Bowman, Meg. *Dramatic Readings on Feminist Issues*, Vol. I. San Jose, CA: Hot Flash Press, 1988.

—— and Haywood, Diane, eds. *Readings for Older Women.* San Jose, CA: Hot Flash Press, 1992.

——. *Readings for Women's Programs.* San Jose, CA: Hot Flash Press, 1984.

Bradley, Marion Zimmer. *The Firebrand.* New York: Simon & Schuster, 1987.

——. *The Mists of Avalon.* New York: Ballantine Books, 1982.

Briffault, Robert. *The Mothers.* London: George Allen & Unwin, 1939.

Brindel, June Rachuy. *Ariadne: A Novel of Ancient Crete.* New York: St. Martin's Press, 1980.

Broude, Norma and Mary D. Garrard, eds. *Feminism and Art History-Questioning the Litany.* New York: Harper & Row, 1982.

Broverman, Inge K., Broverman, D. M., Clarkson, F. E., Rosenkrantz, P. S. and Susan R. Vogel. "Sex Role Stereotypes and Clinical Judgments of Mental Health," *J. of Consulting and Clinical Psychology*, 34, (1970).

Brownmiller, Susan. *Against Our Will: Men, Women and Rape.* New York: Simon & Schuster, 1975.

——*Femininity.* New York: Simon and Schuster, 1984.

Budapest, Z. *The Holy Book of Women's Mysteries.* Berkekey, CA: Wingbow Press, 1989.

Campbell, Joseph. *The Masks of God: Occidental Mythology*, New York: Viking Penguin Inc., 1964.

———. *The Masks of God: Primitive Mythology*. New York: Viking Penguin, Inc., 1976.

Canan, Janine. *She Rises Like the Sun*. Freedom, CA: The Crossing Press, 1989.

Chen, Ellen. "Tao as the Great Mother." *History of Religion,* vol. 51, Spring 1974.

Chernin, Kim. *The Obsession*. New York: Harper & Row, 1981.

Christ, Carol P. *Laughter of Aphrodite*. San Francisco: Harper & Row, 1987.

———. "Why Women Need the Goddess." *Heresies*, Spring 1978.

———. & Plaskow, Judith. *Weaving the Visions*. San Francisco: Harper & Row, 1989.

Cohen, Marcia. *The Sisterhood. New York:* Simon & Schuster, 1988.

Collins, Sheila D. *A Different Heaven and Earth*. Valley Forge, PA: Judson Press, 1974.

Crawford, O. G. S. *The Eye Goddess*. Oak Park, IL: Delphi Press, Inc., 1991.

Daly, Mary. *Beyond God the Father*. Boston: Beacon Press, 1973.

———. *Gyn/Ecology: The Meta-ethics of Radical Feminism*, 2nd edition. Boston, Beacon Press, 1990.

———. *Pure Lust*. Boston: Beacon Press, 1984.

———. *Wickedary*. Boston: Beacon Press, 1987.

Davis, Elizabeth Gould. *The First Sex*. Baltimore: Viking Penguin, 1972.

de Beauvoir, Simone. *The Second Sex*. New York: Bantam Books, 1961.

de Pizan, Christine. *The Book of the City of Ladies*. Trans. E. J. Richards. New York: Persea Books, 1982.

Diamond, Irene and Gloria Feman Orenstein, eds. *Reweaving the World*. San Francisco: Sierra Club Books, 1990.

Dick and Jane as Victims. Princeton, NJ: Women on Words & Images, 1972.

Diner, Helen. *Mothers and Amazons*. Garden City, NY: Anchor Books, 1973.

Dinnerstein, Dorothy. *The Mermain and the Minotaur*. New York: Harper & Row, 1976.

Dobell, Elizabeth Rogers. "God and Woman: The Hidden History." *Redbook*, March 1978.

Ehrenreich, Barbara and Deidre English. *Witches, Midwives and Nurses*. New York: The Feminist Press, 1973.

Eichenbaum, Louise and Susie Orbach, *What Do Women Want*. New York: Coward-McCann Inc., 1983.

Eisler, Riane. *The Chalice and the Blade: Our History, Our Future*. San Francisco: Harper & Row, 1987.

Engel, J. Ronald and Joan Gibb Engel, eds. *Ethics of Environment and Development*. Tucson: University of Arizona Press, 1990.

Engelsman, Joan. *The Feminine Dimension of the Divine*. Philadelphia: Westminster Press, 1979.

Fahs, Sophia. *Today's Children and Yesterday's Heritage*. Boston: Beacon Press, 1952.

Faludi, Susan. *Backlash* New York: Anchor Books/Doubleday, 1991.

Fischer, Clare B. *Breaking Through: A Bibliography of Women and Religion*. Berkeley, CA: Graduate Theological Union Library, 1980.

Fosdick, Harry Emerson. *A Guide to Understanding the Bible*. New York: Harper Brothers, 1958.

French, Marilyn. *The Women's Room*. New York: Ballantine Books, 1977.

Frazer, James. *The Golden Bough: A Study in Magic and Religion*. New York, Macmillan Publishing Company, 1922.

Gadon, Elinor. *The Once and Future Goddess*. San Francisco: Harper & Row, 1989.

Gage, Matilda Joslyn. *Woman, Church and State*. Watertown, MA: Persephone Press, 1980.

Getty, Adele. *Goddess*. London: Thames & Hudson Ltd., 1990.

Gilligan, Carol. *In A Different Voice: Psychological Theory and Women's Development*. Cambridge, MA: and London: Harvard University Press, 1982.

Gimbutas, Marija. *Gods and Goddesses of Old Europe, 7000-3500 B.C.: Myths, Legends and Cult Images*. Berkeley, CA: University of California Press, 1974.

———. *The Language of the Goddess*. Harper & Row, San Francisco, 1989.

"Girls Talk; Boys Talk More," *The Harvard Education Letter*, Vol. 7, No. 1, Jan./Feb., 1991, Cambridge, MA.

Gleason, Judith. *Oya, In Praise of the Goddess*. Boston: Shambhala, 1987.

Goldenberg, Naomi. *Changing of the Gods*. Boston: Beacon Press, 1979.

Gore, Al *Earth in the Balance: Ecology and the Human Spirit*. New York: Houghton-Mifflin Company, 1992.

Graves, Robert. *The White Goddess*. New York,: Farrar, Strauss & Giroux, 1948.

Gray, Elizabeth Dodson. *Patriarchy as a Conceptual Trap*. Wellesley, MA· Roundtable Press, 1982.

Greenberg, Blu. *On Women and Judaism*. Philadelphia: The Jewish Publication Society of America, 1981.

Griffin, Susan. *Woman and Nature*. San Francisco: Harper & Row, 1978.

———. *Unremembered Country*. Port Townsend, WA: Copper Canyon Press, 1987.

Gross, Rita, ed. *Beyond Androcentrism: New Essays on Women and Religion*. Missoula, MT: Scholars Press, 1977.

Hallo, W.W. and J.A.A. Van Dijk, trans. *The Exaltation of Inanna*. New Haven: Yale University Press, 1968.

Harrison, Jane Ellen. *Prologomena to the Study of Greek Religion*. Cambridge: Cambridge University Press, 1922.

Hawkes, Jacquetta. *The World of the Past*. Vol. I & Vol. II. New York Simon & Schuster, 1963.

Hawthorne, Nan. *Loving the Goddess Within*. Oak Park, IL: Delphi Press Inc., 1991.

Horney, Karen. *Feminine Psychology*. New York: W. W. Norton & Co. Inc., 1967.

Jade. *To Know*. Oak Park, IL: Delphi Press Inc., 1991.

Julian of Norwich. *Enfolded in Love*. London: 1980.

———. *Revelations of Divine Love*. Trans. by C. Wolters, Middlesex, England: Penguin Books, 1966.

Kane, Herb Kawainui. *Pele*. Captain Cook, HI: The Kawainui Press, 1987.

Keller, Catherine. *From a Broken Web*. Boston: Beacon Press, 1986.

Kerenyi, K. *Archetypal Image of Mother and Daughter*. Princeton, NJ: Bollingen Series, Princeton University Press, 1967.

Kinstler, Clysta. *The Moon Under Her Feet*. San Francisco: Harper San Francisco, 1989.

Klein, Tzipora. *Celebrating Life*. Oak Park, IL: Delphi Press Inc., 1992.

Krupnick, Catherine. "Women and Men in the Classroom: Inequality and its Remedies." *On Teaching and Learning: Journal of the Harvard Danforth Center*, Spring, 1985.

Langdon, S. *Tammuz and Ishtar*. Oxford: Clarendon Press, 1914.

Laura, Judith. *She Lives! The Return of Our Great Mother*. Freedom, CA: The Crossing Press, 1989.

Lederer, Laura, ed. *Take Back the Night*. New York: William Morrow & Co. Inc., 1980.

Lerner, Gerda. *Black Women in White America*. New York: Random House, 1972.

——. *The Creation of Patriarchy*. Oxford University Press, New York, 1986.

Levy, Rachel. *The Gate of Horn: Religious Conceptions of the Stone Age and Their Influence on European Thought*. London: Faber and Faber Ltd., 1948.

Lifshin, Lyn, ed. *Tangled Vines: A Collection of Mother and Daughter Poems*. Boston: Beacon Press, 1976.

Lipman-Blumen. *Gender Roles and Power*. Englewood Cliffs, NJ: Prentiss-Hall Inc., 1984.

McDade, Carolyn. *Honor Thy Womanself: A Song Book*. Boston: Unitarian Universalist Women's Federation, 1974.

Mark, Teressa. *She Changes*. Oak Park, IL: Delphi Press Inc., 1991.

Martz, Sandra, ed. *When I Am An Old Woman I Shall Wear Purple*. Watsonville, CA: Papier-Mache Press, 1987.

Mascetti, Manuela Dunn. *The Song of Eve*. New York: Simon & Schuster, 1990.

Miller, Beth, ed. *Women in Hispanic Literature*. Berkeley, CA: University of California Press, 1983.

Miller, Jean Baker. *Toward a New Psychology of Women*. Boston: Beacon Press, 1976.

Monaghan, Patricia. *Dictionary of Goddesses and Heroines*, 2nd edition. Minneapolis, MN, Llewellyn Publications, 1990.

———. *Seasons of the Witch*. Oak Park, IL: Delphi Press Inc., 1992.

Morgan, Elaine. *The Descent of Woman*. New York: Stein & Day, 1972.

Morgan, Robin. *The Anatomy of Freedom*. Garden City, NY: Anchor Press/Doubleday, 1982.

———, ed. *Sisterhood is Powerful*. New York: Random House, 1970.

Morris, Joan. *The Lady Was a Bishop: The Hidden History of Women with Clerical Ordination and the Jurisdiction of Bishops*. New York: Macmillan, 1973.

Morton, Nelle. *The Journey Is Home*. Beacon Press, Boston, 1985.

Neumann, Erich. *The Great Mother*. Princeton University Press, Bolloingen Series, 1972.

Ochs, Carol. T*he Myth Behind the Sex of God: Toward a New Consciousness Transcending Matriarchy and Patriarchy*. Boston: Beacon Press, 1977.

O'Flagherty, Wendy Doniger. *Women, Androgynes, and Other Mythical Beasts*. Chicago: University of Chicago Press, 1980.

Orbach, Susie. *Fat is a Feminist Issue*. New York: Berkeley Books, 1980.

Pagels, Elaine. *Adam, Eve, and the Serpent*. New York: Random House, 1988.

———. *The Gnostic Gospels*. New York: Random House, 1979.

Patai, Raphael. *The Hebrew Goddess*. New York: KTAV {Publishing House, 1967.

Pearson, Carol Lynn. *Mother Wove the Morning*. Video, 1384 Cornwall Ct., Walnut Creek, CA 94596, 1992.

Piercy, Marge. *Fly Away Home*. New York: Fawcett Crest, 1984.

Phillips, Michael and Salli Raspberry. *The Seven Laws of Money*. New York: Random House, 1974.

Ranck, Shirley Ann. *Cakes for the Queen of Heaven*. (Curriculum). Boston: Unitarian Universalist Association, 1986.

Raymond, Janice G. *A Passion for Friends*. Beacon Press, Boston, 1986.

Reed, Evelyn. *Sexism and Science*. New York: Pathfinder Press, 1978.

Reuther, Rosemary Radford. *Sexism and God-Talk*. Boston: Beacon Press, 1983.

———. *New Woman/New Earth*. New York: Random House, 1979.

———, ed. *Religion and Sexism*. New York: Simon & Schuster, 1974.

———. *Womanguides*. Boston: Beacon Press, 1985.

Rosenthal, R. and L. Jacobson. *Pygmalion in the Classroom*. New York: Holt Rinehart & Winston Inc., 1968.

Roszak, B. and T. Roszak, eds. *Masculine/Feminine*. New York: Harper & Row, 1969.

Rufus, Anneli S. and Kristan Lawson. *Goddess Sites: Europe*. San Francisco: Harper San Francisco, 1991.

Rush, Anne Kent. *Moon, Moon*. Berkeley, CA: Moon Books, Random House, 1976.

Sadker, Myra and David Sadker. "Sexism in the Classroom of the 80s." *Psychology Today,* March 1986.

Shaef, Anne Wilson. *Women's Reality.* Minneapolis: Winston Press, 1981.

Sherfey, Mary Jane. *The Nature and Evolution of Female Sexuality.* New York: Vintage Books, 1973.

Seidenberg, Robert and Karen DeCrow. *Women Who Marry Houses.* New York: McGraw-Hill Book Co., 1983.

Sewell, Marilyn, ed. *Cries of the Spirit.* Boston: Beacon Press, 1991.

Shange, Ntosake. *For Colored Girls Who Have Considered Suicide When the Rainbow is Enuf.* New York: Bantam Books, 1980.

Signs. Special Issue on Women and Religion. Vol. 2, no. 2 (Winter 1976).

Sjoo, Monica and Barbara Mor. *The Great Cosmic Mother.* San Francisco: Harper & Row, 1987.

Spender, Dale. *Invisible Women: The Schooling Scandal.* London: Writers and Readers Publishing, 1982.

Spretnak, Charlene. *Lost Goddesses of Early Greece.* Boston: Beacon Press, 1981.

———. *The Spiritual Dimension of Green Politics.* Santa Fe, NM: Bear & Co., 1986.

Stanton, Elizabeth Cady. *The Original Feminist Attack on the Bible.* New York: Arno Press, 1974.

Starhawk. *Dreaming the Dark: Magic, Sex and Politics,* 2nd edition. Boston: Beacon Press, 1988.

———. *The Spiral Dance: The Rebirth of the Ancient Religion of the Great Goddess,* 2nd edition. San Francisco: Harper and Row Publishers, 1989.

———. *Truth or Dare.* San Francisco: Harper & Row, 1987.

Steinen, Gloria. *Outrageous Acts and Everyday Rebellions.* New York: Signet Books, 1986.

——. *The Revolution from Within: A Book of Self Esteem.*

Stone, Merlin. *Ancient Mirrors of Womanhood: A Treasury of Goddess and Heroine Lore from Around the World.* 2nd edition. Boston: Beacon Press, 1991.

——. *When God Was a Woman.* New York: Harcourt, Brace Jovanovich, 1976.

Sumrall, Amber Coverdale and Dena Taylor. *Sexual Harrassment: Women Speak Out,* Freedom, CA: The Crossing Press, 1992.

Tannen, Deborah. *You Just Don't Understand: Women and Men in Conversation.* New York: William Morrow and Company, Inc., 1990.

Teish, Luisah. *Jambalaya.* San Francisco: Harper & Row, 1985.

Teubal, Savina J. *Sarah the Priestess.* Athens, OH: Swallow Press/Ohio University Press, 1984.

Tracy, Denise, ed. *Wellsprings.* Oak Park, IL: Delphi Resources, 1992.

Troeltsch, Ernst. *The Social Teaching of Christian Churches.* Trans. O. Wyon. New York: Harper & Row, 1960.

Truth, Sojourner. *Speech at the Women's Rights Convention,* Akron, Ohio, 1851.

Walker, Alice. *The Color Purple.* New York: Harcourt, Brace Jovanovich, 1982.

Walker, Barbara G. *Amazon.* San Francisco: Harper San Francisco, 1992.

——. *The Crone.* San Francisco: Harper & Row, 1985.

——. *The Woman's Encyclopedia of Myths and Secrets.* San Francisco: Harper and Row, 1983.

———. *Women's Rituals*. San Francisco: Harper & Row, 1990.

Walker, Lenore E. *The Battered Woman*. New York: Harper Colophon Books, 1979.

Warner, Marina. *Alone of All Her Sex*. New York: Simon & Schuster, 1976.

Wells, Theo. "Woman—Which Includes Man of Cource: An Experience in Awareness." San Francisco: *Newsletter for Humanistic Psychology*, December 1970.

Wittig, Monique. *Les Guerrilles*. Trans. David Le Vey. Boston: Beacon Press 1985.

Wolf, Naomi: *The Beauty Myth: How Images of Beauty Are Used Against Women*. New York: William Morrow and Company, inc., 1991.

Wynne, Patrice. *The Womanspirit Sourcebook*. San Francisco: Harper & Row, 1988.

Zipes, Jack. *Don't Bet on the Prince: Contemporary Feminist Fairy Tales in North America and England*. New York: Methuen, 1986.

About the Author

A CRONE OF WISDOM and power who has touched the lives of many women through her writing and teaching, the Reverend Shirley Ann Ranck brings both personal and professional insight to her work. Trained in education, psychology and ministry, she has drawn upon all these disciplines as well as her various personal lives as wife, mother, and single parent to create the female spiritual journey contained in *Cakes for the Queen of Heaven.*

While working full time and birthing and raising two daughters and two sons, Shirley managed to earn her Master's degree in religious education from Drew University, an M.A. in clinical psychology from City College of New York, a Ph.D. in urban school psychology from Fordham University, and her Master of Divinity from Starr King School for the Ministry in Berkeley. She is an educator and a licensed psychologist in California as well as an ordained minister in the Unitarian Universalist Association. She has worked in hospitals, clinics and a county jail for women as well as in private practice.

After many years of service as a Unitarian-Universalist minister, she is now retired and living in the Bay Area where she devotes her time to writing, speaking and being an activist for women's issues and environmental concerns.